The Lyon's Cub

For a moment, time stops. There's nothing but the creak and groan of this Spanish ship, the slap of the water against the hull. Even the cries of the sailors are nothing, nothing. We're alone, he and I, in an unknown wilderness. What will he do? What will he do? I stare at him and he stares back. We're so close I can see the tiny beads of sweat on his forehead, the sprouting of a young man's moustache upon his upper lip. A soldier's uniform but a boy's eyes.

The Lyon's Cub

M.L. Stainer

Illustrated by James Melvin

Chicken Soup Press, Inc.

Circleville, New York

Chicken Soup Press, Inc.
P.O. Box 164
Circleville, NY 10919

Library of Congress Cataloging-in-Publication Data
Stainer, M.L., 1939-
The Lyon's cub / M.L. Stainer ; illustrated by James Melvin
p.   cm. — (The Lyon saga)
Sequel to The Lyon's roar.
Summary: Jessabel, one of the survivors of the disappearance of the English settlers on Roanoake Island in 1587, relates how her remaining companions live with the Croatoan Indians and try to find the missing colonists
ISBN 0-9646904-5-4. —ISBN 0-9646904-6-2 (pbk.)
1. Roanoke Colony (N.C.)—Juvenile fiction. [1. Roanoke Colony (N.C.)—Fiction. 2. Indians of North America — Fiction.]
I. Melvin, James, ill. II. Title. III. Series: Stainer, M.L., 1939- Lyon saga.
PZ7.S78255Lt 1998
[Fic]—dc21   97-47239
                                                          CIP
                                                          AC

Book design by Netherfield Productions, Pine Bush, New York
Printed by Worzalla, Stevens Point, Wisconsin

10 9 8 7 6 5 4 3 2 1

In loving memory of
Alice Ruth Golden

Other Works by M.L. Stainer

The Lyon's Roar (1997)

Contents

Author's Note

The author wishes to note that some spellings of familiar names have been changed according to how they are listed on original documents.

Croatoan is pronounced Cro-ah-tu-WAN; Manteo, MAN-tee-o; Ananyas, An-na-NEE-yus; Akaiyan, Uh-KY-yun; and Towaye, TOH-way.

A special note of thanks to:
Robert Peay and Greg MacAvoy for their proofreading assistance: to Stella Denton of Pine Bush High School library and Fran O'Gorman of Goshen library, for their help in research: to Ricardo Carballal for his invaluable assistance with Spanish: to Harry L. Thompson, Curator of the Port-o-Plymouth Museum, Plymouth, North Carolina, for his encouragement: to my mother, Harriet Stainer, and my friends and family for their continued support.

Tuskeruro dialect: from *A New Voyage to Carolina*, by John Lawson, edited by Hugh Talmadge Lefler. Copyright © 1967 by the University of North Carolina Press. Used by permission of the publisher.

The Names of the 1587 Virginia Colonists: from *The First Colonists: Documents on the Planting of the First English Settlements in North America, 1584-1590*, by David B. Quinn and Alison Quinn. Raleigh: North Carolina Dept. of Cultural Resources, Division of Archives and History, 1982. Used by permission of Oxford University Press.

Prologue

THE CROATOAN INDIANS were known to be friendly to the early colonists, with documented reports of interaction between the English and the Indians. After John White left for England and winter approached, there's a possibility that the colony, feeling abandoned, split in two. Half the colonists may have sailed on the pinnace to the Chesapeake Bay area, to try and establish their *Cittie of Ralegh*. The remaining settlers may have joined with their friendly neighbors, sailing south to Croatoan Island.

It's pure speculation as to what happened. John White didn't reach either Chesapeake Bay or Croatoan Island upon his return in 1590. Storms prevented him from sailing south to where he thought his friends and family were. Instead, his ship returned to England.

Spanish soldiers and explorers ranged throughout the large area of *Virginia* which encompassed the Chesapeake lands, what are now the Carolinas, and all the way to Florida. Their garrison at Chesapeake Bay was called the *Bahía de Santa Maria,* and their ships sailed with regularity up and down the coast. Some of the colonists on Croatoan Island may have attempted to seek out their former friends who headed north, with the intentions of reuniting the two colonies into one. Some may have wished to head inland, no doubt seeking to establish a new colony or perhaps, finding the other half of the original 1587 group.

No one knows for sure.

Chapter 1

Return To Roanoak

TODAY WE LAND AGAIN on Roanoak Island, pulling our canoes up onto its sandy beach. The trip across the water wasn't difficult at all, for the canoes weren't weighted down with our belongings as they'd been when we'd left a year ago.

What a strange feeling it is to set foot upon the land we once claimed as our own. It's overgrown with weeds and a tanglement of vines, much the way it was when we first arrived. Almost a year has passed since we set sail for Croatoan Island that November day, leaving behind our English heritage for the ways of the Indian. It wasn't safe to remain, for Spanish ships were sailing brazenly through the inlet at Hataraske, and from the north fearsome Savages with painted faces moved closer and closer through the woodlands toward our encampment.

Father is with us, not back to his full strength, still coughing. It's become a permanent affliction, I'm afraid. We listen to him cough through the day and into the night, unable to do much to help. The Indians of Croatoan have nursed him back to health, but his lungs are damaged from the illness. It hurts him to breathe deeply of the air needed for life.

This trip to Roanoak excites me. It's a venture of grave undertaking, Father says, to see if John White has returned, to see if it's safe to come back.

"Watch where you step," cautions Ananyas as he leads the way back to the encampment. "It's badly overgrown."

I hear someone curse behind me as he almost trips.

"Look, over here," calls Master Spendlove and we see where he's pointing. Strewn wilfully about the ground are most of John White's possessions, those we'd carefully buried before we left, after promising to safeguard them while he was in England on our behalf.

"The hostiles must have dug them up," says Ananyas with a frown. "They look like they've been lying here for months."

We run over to where he stands. The firearms are rusted from long exposure to the elements, his personal belongings scattered here and there. I give a small cry. All his notes, his carefully-drawn maps and charts, are ruined. Rain has smeared the ink and curled the papers. Nothing is legible. If and when John White returns with our supplies, he won't be pleased to see his belongings in such disrepair.

"Jess, come over here," Father beckons. "I've found something which will please you immensely."

Father and Ananyas are working on a small chest belonging to our governor, which had been sealed before being buried. They've managed to pry it open. Inside are his diary and some official-looking scrolls, his scales and measures, his instruments for drawing. But when Father reaches further, he pulls out sheets and sheets of unused parchment. It's a

2

wondrous discovery!

"These are yours," he says with a smile. "For my young writer."

"Oh, Father," I turn excitedly to him. "Oh, Father, can I... dare I...?"

"Who knows when John White will be returning. Better that you use these sheets than the elements get them."

I hug my beloved father, thinking with joy upon all the writing I'll now be able to do. For my paper ran out ages ago, and I've not been able to write any journal entries for a long time. My original diary lies safe in the small lodge house on Croatoan Island, bound with some of Eleanor's ribbon. I've missed the writings I used to do, having to content myself with reading and re-reading the diary many times throughout the long months which followed. I've grown from a child to a woman and so much has happened since my last entry was made.

"Gather what you can save, what you might need," Ananyas instructs us, and we set about doing just that.

I see Akaiyan watching me as I hug the precious papers to my chest. He's been silent through the whole journey, sitting in the front of our canoe, not saying a single word. I know in my heart he's afraid we'll want to stay on Roanoak, and not return to the home we've made on his island to the south. I know this without his saying it, for I can now read his heart as well as he reads mine.

"Don't be upset," I say to him in fluent Croatoan. "For as you can see, there's nothing here to which we can return."

He nods his head, following me then as I stand before the weed-filled palisade, marking the letters "Croatoan" on the post. I smooth the roughened wood with my fingers, remembering how Ananyas had carved the word so carefully.

3

I feel my eyes brim with tears unleashed by months and months of memories. It's the year of Our Lord 1588, and not a word has come, nor a ship sailed, from England.

Chapter 2

No Sign

AND SO, WE ENTER OUR CANOES and set sail southward, our hearts heavy with sadness. What we'd expected, none of us really knew, perhaps a sign, some sort of indication to let us know that our governor had returned.

Ananyas's face is grim, as is my dear father's, as the men row steadily south. The canoes rise and fall in the swells, heavier now because of the goods we've gathered, but seaworthy, none the less. The men have taken some of the least-rusted firearms, some cooking pots for our women, and sundry items of similar nature. A whole cache of ammunition has been found and confiscated for our use, though most of the men hunt now like our Indian friends, with bow and arrow. Holding the box aloft, Master Spendlove gives a cheer.

"In case our Spanish enemies discover our whereabouts."

But nobody cheers in return. For if the Spanish haven't discovered us, neither have our brave countrymen who, along with John White, pledged to return with supplies and aid.

I sit well back in the canoe, clutching my precious parchment, watching the faces of the others, Indian and Englishman together. I am secretly pleased that Father allowed me to come with them on this excursion, and secretly ashamed that I begged him so. As usual, he'd been reluctant to take me along; as usual, it was Ananyas who pointed out that I could help gather those items I thought our women might need. Mother, of course, had been against the idea. How strange, that once she'd been against my going to Croatoan Island so many months ago and now, the exact opposite.

"I'm not a child," I said to her with a firmness that startled even me.

"Indeed," she remarked quietly. "You are more Indian than anything."

I tried to see if she were angry but sensed, instead, only a sadness deeper than her usual demeanor. For try as she might to keep me to my English ways, I was rapidly becoming more and more an Indian maiden.

Akaiyan is watching the waters ahead. The troubled look upon his face has vanished. The closer we get to his beloved home, the more he relaxes. Father is silent; even his cough is stilled. I wonder what thoughts race through his mind. For he'd pledged to build us a new life in this wilderness, to make of it a home, and our home is not a strong-timbered house in a community of Englishmen, but a brush lodge in the middle of an Indian village.

I'm almost sixteen and know now, in reflecting back, that my dear beloved Father will never be the same man he once was. He's aged terribly from his illness, with much gray streaking his hair and beard. He's thinner and doesn't have the strength I remember. But he's alive and well, and seems

6

content to walk and read the Holy Bible. He loves to play with Virginia and watches Eleanor teach the little Indian children. There's a weariness about him which he wears like a mantle upon his shoulders. Only with the babe does it lift and I see once more, the carefree father of my childhood.

Ah, my childhood. I had a dream about George Howe the other night. Strange that I haven't dreamed about him in many months. He came to me like a shadow from my past, brushed my lips with his in a tender kiss and then, was gone. I reached out to grab his substance, but my hands slipped through mist. I awoke with my eyes wet from tears.

George Howe would be almost nineteen by now. Perhaps he'd be wed already, with a child. I try to picture George with a wife and family in Chesapeake, but it's hard. For whom would he have married? Sweet Agnes, who now lies buried back on Roanoak, and myself, were the only young girls on our original pilgrimage. My hand flies to my mouth. Perhaps George, like I with Akaiyan, has met a young Indian woman. Perhaps he has wed her. But then I shake my head. No, that's impossible. George was much too English to consider marriage to an Indian. He hated the thought that I was so drawn to them. How it used to bother him!

I'm deep in these thoughts of George as our canoe scrapes the rough sand of Croatoan Island. Mother is there to greet us at the beach, clapping her hands in delight at seeing us all safe and sound. Mistress Steueens exclaims loudly and joyfully over the cooking pots and utensils. Akaiyan pulls the canoes high onto the shore. He nods his head in a silent greeting of respect for my mother, who nods in return. Father walks over and embraces her.

"And what news?" she asks in a tremulous voice.

"All is as we left it," he sighs.

"No sign of our governor, then?"

"Not one."

"Mother, the hostiles got to his belongings and dug them up. All his maps and possessions were strewn about...."

She gives a sob, burying her face in her hands. Father holds her tightly.

"Don't fear," he says. "John White will come, I know it."

"But when?"

And her question is one we've all been asking. Leaning her head upon his shoulder, they walk together up the beach. Once more, the rest of us gather the goods from Roanoak and follow them, toward the village and our life with the Indians.

Chapter 3

The Plan

"AND WHAT DOES THIS MEAN?" Eleanor Dare asks Ananyas. "My father told us he'd return within the year."

She watches her babe Virginia toddle toward him, arms outstretched. Ananyas swoops her up before she falls, and whirls her around the room. Virginia giggles in delight. Eleanor's eyes light up, but the lines of worry are still around her mouth.

"Do you think the Spanish ships have sunk his fleet?"

Ananyas shakes his head.

"It's more likely that he hasn't even sailed. Our good Queen Elizabeth is probably battling Philip's Armada right now...."

"...If that's the case," Father interrupts, "then no English ships will sail with supplies for us until the war's ended."

Eleanor stifles a sob.

"But... how will we manage?"

Father looks grim-faced at Ananyas.

"My dearest," says Ananyas, giving her Virginia and kneeling by her side. "We'll manage as we've already done, living with our Indian friends and working the soil, hunting...."

Eleanor thrusts the babe at me and runs from the room. We sit in silence broken only by Virginia's cooing, as each of us contemplates our future. For Eleanor, it is doubly worse, for John White is the father she may never see again.

Mother is equally unhappy with the news. But with my brother Thomas around, she catches herself, steeling her shoulders and making ready the supper meal.

"Give your mother a hand," Father says and so I do, setting the makeshift table with proper English plates and utensils that we've rescued from Roanoak just the day before. Though I, like Thomas, never minded eating with my fingers as our Indian friends, I know Mother will delight in being able to use tableware again.

"What does it mean?" Akaiyan asks me after our supper is finished, the table cleared and we are able to be alone. Father and Mother are still inside, no doubt talking with Eleanor and Ananyas, as Akaiyan and I watch the sun lower in the western sky and night fall upon us.

"Our governor, John White, was to bring back supplies and more men. He told us he'd be back within one year."

"There was no sign of people at your camp."

I shake my head sorrowfully.

"No. It's just as we left it last November. We left him a marker if he returned, so he'd know where to look for us."

"Little Bird," Akaiyan takes my hand. "Are you unhappy living here with us?"

"No," I say honestly. "I'm at peace and content to live among the Croatoan."

"But your family...? The others...?"

"John White is Eleanor's father, like Manteo is yours. She misses him. They all miss the English ways."

Akaiyan stares at me.

"And you?"

I don't answer for a minute, then laugh and dart away.

"Am I not a good Indian maiden. Look at my clothing, look at my feet."

And, indeed, it's true. For I am wearing clothes of buckskin, not homespun cloth, and soft moccasins they call *oo-ross-soo*.

"Am I not a good Indian maiden?" I ask again. Akaiyan still doesn't answer. I can see he's puzzled.

"You... are happy. They... are not."

"I'm at peace," I finally answer.

"Is that... happy?"

"*Kawa* - today I'm happy."

"And *jureha?*"

"Who knows what tomorrow will bring."

Father calls me then and I turn to go. Akaiyan grabs my hand and holds me back.

"Little Bird, tomorrow will you be happy also?"

I look into his deep brown eyes.

"When I am with you, I'm happy. I'm happy with the *unqua.*"

He watches me go and I leave a part of my heart behind with him, as I enter the lodge house of my parents.

"Well, it's decided then," I hear Ananyas say, slapping his hand upon the table. In the corner, Eleanor is weeping quietly.

"What's decided, Father?"

He gives a deep sigh, then a spasm of coughing seizes him.

"They're going to the Chesapeake to find the others. They're not going to wait for John White to return."

"Thomas, hush," says Mother quickly. She shoos him outside to wash before bedtime.

"Who's going to Chesapeake?" I ask. Father doesn't answer.

"Who's going to....?"

"I am," says Ananyas in a firm voice. "I and several of the men. We're going to find the rest of our good people. If all's well, we'll return for you and join once more as a colony."

"But how will you get there? They took our pinnace."

"The Croatoan will lend us a canoe."

Mother sits down next to Eleanor, placing her arm about Eleanor's shoulders.

"Sad as you might be, my dear, this is a good decision. You can't stay here, none of us can, raising little Virginia as an... Indian."

I want to cry out, why not, what's wrong with living as an Indian? But I bite my tongue. No one would understand how I feel. I turn to my father.

"Who's going, Father? Are you?"

"Indeed, I'd like to go, but my health won't permit it. No, Ananyas, Master Spendlove, Thomas Steeuens and an Indian guide." He stares at me. "Only men, my dear Jess. This isn't a good venture for a young woman."

"I don't want to go anyway," I say in a sudden fit of temper. "I don't want to go. I want to stay here."

Mother looks sadly over at Father.

"Only Jess appears content here," he says then with a sigh. "Only my dear daughter, who is turning into an Indian before my very eyes...."

12

Chapter 4

Setting Sail

HOW QUICKLY THE PREPARATIONS are made for Ananyas and the other men to leave! Supplies have been gathered, the canoe readied and all too soon, the day comes for their departure.

Their plan is to sail once more across the sound toward Roanoak. But instead of landing upon the southern shore, they'll continue up its coastline and beyond, all the way to the mainland. From there, they'll shoulder the canoe and travel as far north as they can. Then once more into the canoe, crossing the broad Baye of Chesapeake to where our colonists are supposed to be.

It won't be an easy journey, Father says. Carrying the canoe overland will be an arduous task. Also, there are other dangers: Spanish soldiers, and the hostile tribes of Powhatan which freely roam the northern woodlands, hunting for food or whatever else they can find.

"Why not sail through the Hataraske inlet into the outer

sea, and ride the coastline that way?"

"Because, my dear Jess, the waters of the mighty ocean are treacherous along these shores. The canoe would be dashed against the shoals. And besides, Spain sails her ships brazenly along that route, and they'd be sighted easily."

During this time of preparation, Eleanor remains downcast. I don't blame her. Ananyas will be gone many weeks. It will be their first separation since leaving England. Mother tries to console her but oftentimes, I catch her silently weeping as she watches Virginia playing with a toy.

On the final day, the men stock the canoe with the barest minimum of supplies. They'll live off the land, Father tells us, hunting their food, gathering berries and nuts. Using the maps of John White which are still legible, Ananyas has carefully drawn his own route, marking their departure from Croatoan Island, to Roanoak, then across the wilderness toward that big body of water, the Baye of Chesapeake. He studies the map over and over again, conferring with the guide, Skotai, and the others who venture forth also. There is much discussion.

Amidst tears and with heavy hearts, we bid our small brave group a sad farewell. Eleanor has refused to come down to the beach to see them off. Ananyas lingers long in their lodge house. His face is grim when he leaves to meet the others. Mother comes also, but she hangs back, her mouth drawn in a thin, tight smile.

"Too many goodbyes," she says in great pain. She turns then and walks back toward the village. But Father and I, Thomas, Mistress Steueens and some others, as well as Manteo and Akaiyan, fix our gazes upon the small canoe as they row away, until we can see it no longer.

"Come," says Father, his arm about my shoulder.

"Come, sweet Jess. You must go to comfort Eleanor, for her nights will be lonely."

"I'm sore afraid for them," sighs Mistress Steueens, wringing her hands together. She picks up a corner of her apron and wipes her eyes.

"What do you think they'll find, Father, when they reach Chesapeake?"

"Why, our friends and neighbors," he says with a laugh. "And your favorite, young George Howe."

I don't answer, thinking of George as I remember him that last day back on Roanoak, weeping openly as he begged me to go with him. The pain in my heart when he left was like a knife, sharp and terrible. But the passage of months has done its work well, easing that pain to a dull ache, then to a soft, hazy remembrance. Just ahead of me now walks one who has filled that empty space, in such a manner that my heartbeat echoes his, my longing to be a part of his people consumes my very soul.

Father sees me staring at Akaiyan and tightens his grip on my shoulders.

"Let's hope our men find the other colonists and return soon, so we may all move from here..."

Chapter 5

The Long Wait

"THE NIGHTS ARE SO LONELY, I have trouble sleeping."

Eleanor and I are sitting together outside the lodge house that Ananyas, along with our Indian friends, helped construct for them.

"I listen to Virginia's breathing, but it's the only sound I can hear."

I reach out to touch her hand. She glances at me.

"I even miss his snoring."

Then we both laugh, but her laughter quickly fades and melancholy sweeps across her features.

"It's been two weeks now. Do you suppose they're all right?"

"Of course they are," I answer quickly. My own fears must be kept hidden from her, Father has cautioned me several times. Even with one of Manteo's brave warriors as their guide, we know the perils: the danger from Spaniards and the hostiles, and the slim chance of finding their way to our friends in Chesapeake. This is the first time she's asked this question. Perhaps my reply is too glib, for she stares at me long and hard.

"This one who goes with them, is he a good scout?"

"Akaiyan says that Skotai is excellent. He'll do whatever's necessary to avoid danger."

"But there are too many dangers...." Her voice trails off. She offers little Virginia a small piece of fruit. I thank our good Lord for her babe, who brings such joy to her life and ours. No matter how much distress we may feel, just one look at that sweet little girl, walking now with more assurance, is enough to bring a smile to our faces.

When I have a chance later that day, I ask Father how long he thinks it will be before they return. He sighs deeply.

"We've no way of knowing, Jess. We can only estimate a period of several weeks. It depends upon many things."

"Have you ever gone that far north?" I question Akaiyan as he sits stringing another bow.

"My father and I have traveled as far as one moon's passage," he answers. "The woodlands are thick and we crossed many *ahunt wackena*."

"What did you see besides trees and rivers?"

"Some *squarrena*."

I gasp.

"Wolves? How many?"

He smiles.

"How do you say it, a few? We traveled with *hothooka* in our faces, the Northwest-Wind. The wolves were hungry and looking for food. They ran away when they saw us. I was not *werricauna*."

"Is Skotai a good guide?"

Akaiyan nods.

"My father chose him especially for his skills. He can read even one single star, *uttewiraratse*, and know where he is."

I run to tell Eleanor what Akaiyan has told me. She listens without saying a word. Then she gives me a surprising hug and a soft kiss upon my cheek.

The days pass slowly for sweet Eleanor and Mistress Steueens, quickly for me. I keep busy helping Eleanor teach the children, cooking and sewing with my dear mother, bringing drinks of clear sweet water to those who are thirsty. I see little of my brother, Thomas. He's growing so rapidly that we've had to make him Indian clothes also, for we have no English homespun to cut and sew for new trousers. Mother sighs when she sees him clad in buckskin like the *unqua*. He wants to cut his hair in the style of Akaiyan and the other young Croatoan braves. Mother has forbidden it.

It's during this time of waiting for news that I do a great deal of writing. Those precious sheets of parchment are put to good use. While little Virginia naps each afternoon, I'm able to write my innermost thoughts down on paper, listening to her rhythmic breathing, giving Eleanor some time alone. She usually goes for walks near the village, for she likes to have private moments. I know that's when she says her prayers for the safe return of Ananyas and the others.

I start my new journal by telling all that's happened since we first landed on Croatoan Island. The death of Manteo's mother, Shanewis, came just a week after we arrived.

"You must hurry," Akaiyan called and I rushed from our lodge house to see Shanewis breathe her last. Such sadness surrounded us then, when Shanewis's essence left her body to be with the Great Spirit. Manteo beat his chest and cut his arms in grief, the blood running down his wrists. Mother turned her face away for she couldn't bear to see. But I watched and when Akaiyan did the same, made a healing paste to apply later.

Shanewis was the leader of the tribe of Croatoans and for a time, they were without guidance. But then her sister Sinopa claimed her right, and took Shanewis's place. Sinopa was a good leader, and because she wasn't as old as Shanewis, the tribe knew they'd be content under her guidance for many seasons.

Akaiyan explained that the Croatoans were ruled by women in this matriarchal society. It was a good thing, he said, freeing the men for hunting and gathering without warring among themselves for seniority and privilege.

"Women are the bearers of life," he said, "the daughters of Mother Earth, and through them flows the seed of the tribe. It is only natural that they should rule."

I confess I found it to be a simple and perfectly normal occurrence. For wasn't the England we'd left behind also ruled by our beloved Queen Elizabeth, wielding her power with compassion and a woman's true strength? I didn't question Akaiyan when he explained all this, applying the healing mixture I'd made to his arms. Nor did I flinch at his grieving cuts. From all I'd seen since first setting sail from England, the sight of this blood no longer scared me.

Chapter 6

The Healing

AKAIYAN AND MANTEO STAYED in mourning for Shanewis for several weeks. But I couldn't remain sad that long. I hadn't known Shanewis well, only to listen to some of her stories as I tried to learn more about the Indians.

The day Shanewis died, I turned fifteen. It was December twelfth in the year 1587. So as not to anger our Indian friends, we held a small and very private ceremony to mark the occasion in the lodge house Manteo had given us. Mother gave me a hug and her silver locket. I cried when she put it around my neck. Eleanor presented me with a scarf she'd kept hidden those many months. It was blue and silver, matching the locket to perfection. My brother Thomas gave me a wood carving he'd made, beaming with much pride. My beloved Father who, at that time, was still suffering from the ague, couldn't join in our merriment, but held my hand to his lips and kissed my palm. The tears in my eyes, I assured him, were because of the silver locket and the beautiful scarf. I

21

strangled a sob as he coughed into the handkerchief, that incessant cough which racked him so. Mother bit her lip 'til the blood came but, skilled at subterfuge, smiled as she brought his honey tea and herbal medicine.

We sat quietly through most of that evening, listening to the keening of the tribe as the women washed Shanewis' body, in readiness for her trip to the spirit world. At one point, Mother put her hands over her ears, but whether it was to block out the lamentations or Father's coughing, I couldn't tell. The smoke from the lodge fire filled the rafters, so Mother insisted that Father get up and go outside with her. We all helped him up, my poor dear Father, once so strong and now so weak. The cold fresh air cleared our heads and we stayed outside for as long as we could, until another bout of spasms shook his frame.

"Take me inside," he insisted weakly. That night we slept fitfully, half-listening to the wailing and chanting well into the next morning. When I awoke, I was fifteen and my father lay coughing still. I listened to the keening outside and my own heart stirred with sorrow for all I'd left behind.

A special healing ceremony was held soon after for my beloved father. Towaye gathered more roots and herbs, brewing them into yet another of his foul concoctions. Once more, my poor father was made to drink a vile, blackish liquid which I could smell from where I sat across the room. He choked and heaved mightily, but Towaye just gave him more. The sheet was covered with black vomit which spewed from his lips. But at last Towaye was satisfied that he had, indeed, retained a goodly portion.

Then Towaye began chanting strange incantations that I couldn't understand. From beneath his cloak he produced a snake of great proportions. Mother gasped, her hands flying to her mouth. I drew back in fear for the snake was, indeed, alive and writhing.

"Oh, pray stop him," Mother begged Ananyas. But before he could move, Akaiyan placed a warning hand on his arm.

"There is nothing to fear. The snake's poison has been removed."

Nonetheless, Mother was ready to intervene herself but stopped when she heard the warning rattle of the tail. She stood as a statue watching in horror and, like the rest of us *nickreruroh*, Englishmen, was powerless to move. Towaye then held the snake high and uttered several loud chants which I couldn't make out. He bent over my father and wrapped the snake around his chest. The snake wriggled but couldn't escape. Towaye bound the snake tightly to my father's chest with strips of hide so that it couldn't move. Its rattles whirred unceasingly. Akaiyan whispered,

"The evil in your father's chest will enter the *us-quauh-ne*, for that is where it belongs. It cannot bite him. Towaye has sucked out the poison and removed its fangs."

Mother swooned at that point and Ananyas caught her and laid her upon the bed. We watched as Towaye placed a small container filled with hot coals on the floor by my father's bed. He swiftly constructed a make-shift canopy and draped heavy bearskins over all, my father, the captive snake and the smoldering coals. Akaiyan led me out then, along with Ananyas and the others. I wanted to stay but he said it was now between the good spirit, or *quera*, and the bad spirit. In the morning, we would know.

"The snake should be *whaharia*," he said. "The evil spirit will slip back into it."

"I wouldn't want my father to be *whaharia*," I answered

in a choking voice. "Are you sure it's the snake working or the potion Towaye gave him?"

Akaiyan smiled.

"Both," he answered, leading me from the lodge. "And the heat from the coals. We will know *jureha*."

"When *jureha* comes, I hope to greet my dear father once more," and I ran quickly from him into the woods, where I wept and said my prayers most intently, both in English and Croatoan as Akaiyan had taught me.

For three nights, Towaye alone kept a vigil by my father's bed. Mother wasn't allowed near, not even Manteo. Mother was sure Towaye was an evil witch doctor bent on doing Father grievous harm.

We went about our daily activities with a dull heart, eyes looking always toward our lodge where Father slept. Each night we could hear Towaye's incantations and, on occasion, a low moan from my father's lips. Then, on the third night, Mother was allowed in. I heard her scream and ran to the lodge house, only to bump into Towaye leaving.

"Your father is better," he said in Croatoan. "*Utta-ana-wox.*"

"I'll fetch some food right away," I replied and delivered a plate of hot venison stew to my mother.

"How is he?"

She smiled a thin smile.

"He's better. I can't believe it. He's sitting up but tired, so very tired still."

I gave her a hug and a kiss.

"What about the snake?"

She shuddered.

"That horrible thing! It's dead, thank the Good Lord. Towaye has taken it off and buried it somewhere."

She gave me a strange look.

"Now don't say it was an evil spirit which entered the snake and thus, cured your father."

I shrugged my shoulders.

"The Indians have strange ways, Mother, but I suspect it was probably the herbal potion and the sweating heat. Does he still cough?"

"He hasn't in quite a while. His lungs seem clear enough." She smiled. "If you want to believe in spirits, I suppose you may. It's just that I...."

I ran on flying feet to Akaiyan.

"My father's better. He's sitting up and eating."

Akaiyan nodded his head.

"The *quera* is strong for our people. Towaye has good medicine."

"What did he do with the *us-quauh-ne?*"

"He buried it deep in the woods, far away from our village. But first, he said many prayers so that the evil remains locked inside its body."

I nodded in return.

"The Croatoan are good people and that's why the *quera* is so strong."

We looked at each other and suddenly laughed.

Chapter 7

Bad News

I'VE FILLED MANY SHEETS OF PAPER with my entries, trying to record everything that happened during our first year with Manteo's tribe. Father is well enough now though, of course, his cough lingers. Even Mother has conceded that their *quera* is strong. She laughs when she says this.

"Imagine, an Englishwoman believing in such things!"

But even she is becoming more like an Indian wife. Her two children wear clothes of buckskin and speak in the Croatoan tongue whenever they can. Her own shoes wore out a long time ago, and she now slips her feet into *oo-ross-soo* and covers our beds at night with bearskin blankets.

Only Eleanor holds onto the ways of our English countrymen, refusing to dress little Virginia in soft deerskin clothing. Instead, she unravels the tiny sweaters which are now outgrown and re-knits them into a larger size. There'll come a time when she can't do this any longer, and I tell her so. She just shakes her head and bends once more to the task before her.

"I think Eleanor is holding on to the old ways because Ananyas hasn't returned," I tell Akaiyan. He's teaching me how to hold the bow and shoot arrows at a target. I'm so clumsy, but he's very patient. My arms are growing tired from pulling the sinew taut.

"When will they return?" I ask him knowing, of course, that he hasn't the answer.

And then, all too soon, the news comes upon us and it's bad, so very bad.

Skotai has returned to our camp. Leaning upon him, limping and with clothing torn and bloodied, is Thomas Steueens. They're alone.

"Father, come quickly," Thomas calls, the first to spot them emerging from the trees near the beach. We all go running.

"Here, let me take him," says Mistress Steueens, pushing boldly forward. Her brave husband collapses upon the earth. She wipes the sweat from his face, patting his arms, his shoulders, bestowing kiss upon kiss. He smiles weakly.

"And what of the others?" Father asks Skotai. Manteo turns to him and Skotai talks so fast, I can't even follow. There's much gesturing and pantomiming. I quickly gather that they were attacked from behind, caught unawares and, horror of horrors, Ananyas and Master Spendlove were killed.

Father's face is set in a grimace of pain. He helps Master Steueens to his feet, allowing him to lean heavily upon his shoulder. Mistress Steueens walks behind, sobbing profusely. Manteo and Skotai are still talking. I can't speak, but only choke on my own tears.

Ananyas dead! Surely that can't be true! Oh, how will we tell sweet Eleanor? What will she say? What will she do? I dread our approach to the village. Even my brother hangs back, reluctant to be the first to enter the circle of lodge houses.

Father beckons Thomas and me over. He pulls us to one side and whispers urgently,

"Say nothing to anyone, not even Mother. Promise!"

We both nod our heads. Thomas runs near the clearing and begins to dig furiously in the dirt. Though still young, he understands the horror of the situation. As for me, I turn to the only solace I can think of, Akaiyan, who holds out his hand. I reach to touch him, to cling to him in my grief and sorrow.

Father goes somberly into our lodge house. I hear my dear mother gasp, then begin to weep. Roger Bayley comes over, as do others. Even the men have tears running down their cheeks.

Where is Eleanor? Why hasn't she heard any of this? And then I see her, walking through the field toward the village, little Virginia running and dancing around her. I gasp. Who will tell her? Who?

There's so much sadness, I can't even write. It's taken me some time to clear my head enough to put this all down on paper. It's the only way I have to deal with my grief. Father called Eleanor to our lodge and both he and Mother told her the heartbreaking news. We expected screams of anguish, but there weren't any. Eleanor swooned upon hearing the news and Mother put her to bed in our house. One of the other women took little Virginia to stay overnight. Eleanor stayed in our lodge for two days, then gathered her child and went to where she and Ananyas dwelt. She remained inside for several days. Only Mother went to visit, bringing hot soup and caring for the babe. She wouldn't allow Mother to stay overnight.

"It's terrible," Mother said. "She just sits in the chair Ananyas carved and rocks little Virginia on her lap. She barely eats enough to feed a sparrow. When the babe is tired, she climbs herself upon the cot and falls asleep, sucking her thumb. Eleanor doesn't even seem to notice."

Several of our women have tried to coax her out to join them in a meal. They offer to take Virginia into their houses. But Eleanor clutches the little girl and shakes her head. The whole village mourns, including our Indian friends. The women of the tribe have tried also to entice her to eat, to take Virginia, but Eleanor refuses all.

From what we learned from Skotai, their group was about to camp for the night. They were set upon in their sleep by a band belonging to Powhatan's tribe. There was barely time to raise a shout of warning. Ananyas took an arrow to the heart and fell immediately. Master Spendlove was shot as he tried to run. Only Skotai and Thomas Steueens were able to escape and this, because Skotai killed two of the hostiles and Master Steueens shot the other two with his firearm after receiving several wounds.

Mother sits weeping quietly as we are told what happened.

"Did they have a Christian burial?"

"Indeed," replies Thomas Steueens. "Skotai and I dug their graves ourselves. We placed crosses above them. But we couldn't linger. It was then that we decided to return."

"The wisest thing you could have done," Father says. He coughs and reaches for a cup of water.

"Did you say prayers over them?" Mother asks.

Thomas Steueens nods.

"I regret," he says, the tears streaming down his face, "that I couldn't bring their bodies home with us."

Mother buries her face in her hands.

"My poor Eleanor," she keeps saying over and over. "First her father, now Ananyas."

Chapter 8

In Mourning

I LEARN MUCH FROM THE INDIANS during this terrible mourning period. Akaiyan's people are similar to us in their belief in a heaven and hell. He explains to me about their concept of immortality of the soul. He says that when the soul departs from the body, it goes either to heaven which is the habitat of the gods, or to a great pit or hole, there to burn continuously. That place they call *popogusso*, the furthest part of the world toward the sunset. Which direction the soul takes depends on the life's work it has done.

"Your friends are with all the gods," he tells me, showing me the images of some of their gods which he calls *kewasowok*. They're carved in the form of men.

"We have but one God," I tell him, my voice still raw from sobbing.

"We, too," he says most solemnly. "The one chief and great God we can not speak of... except to call him Great Spirit. But he created many lesser gods to help him in ruling our world."

"We have only one God," I repeat stubbornly. "It's hard for me to understand the need for so many."

Akaiyan puts his hand on my arm.

"We are not so different...," he says, searching for the words to express himself. "You give thanks for the rain, for a day in which the sun is warm, for crops to grow. We do, also, understanding... that our gods flow from the Great Spirit who created all things."

I sit in the dark for many nights, listening to Eleanor's soft weeping, for Mother has sent me to stay with her as a sister, and she has allowed it. The babe Virginia whimpers in her sleep. Sometimes she wakes with a cry, then settles back down when I rub her back. I sit in the dark with only the fire's glow to mark the shadows, and think of what Akaiyan has tried to explain; many gods, one God, all intermingling and flowing into each other. My heart is weary and burdened with pain, for Eleanor's deep loss and the loss of any and all our good men. Great black circles have formed under my eyes.

I say to Eleanor,

"You must eat, please, won't you eat something," but she shakes her head.

"This isn't good," Mother says one day and, surprising all of us, marches into Eleanor's house with a plate of stew.

What she says to her is private between the two of them, but after that Eleanor begins eating again and we all breathe a great sigh of relief.

Manteo himself bids me walk in the woodlands with him, speaking in Croatoan for he knows how well I understand. He speaks of life and its sweetness, of death and its peacefulness. And when he speaks of our great loss, he mentions Shanewis, his mother, and his wife who died in childbirth.

"I watched you, Little Bird," he says in his deep musical voice. "All those days while we were upon the waters. You were special. I saw in you what was good and beautiful growing before my eyes. But you had so much fear in you. You ran away from Manteo."

I nod my head, remembering how foolish I'd been.

"But then you were not afraid, for you began to know and understand." He pauses. "Death is like that. What we do not understand, we fear. There is no fear in you now for the *unqua* ways?"

"No," I answer. "Your ways are beautiful."

"Death is just another path the spirit takes. We are part of all this," and he waves his hand to touch the earth, the sky. "Have no more fear of dying. Go and be at peace in your heart."

And I am.

Chapter 9

What To Do?

OUR ENGLISH GROUP MOVES in a daze within the Indian village. The men look weary and their faces are tired and drawn. They do their work with heavy hearts. The women weep openly when they're with each other, wiping their eyes as they pass Eleanor's lodge house. They're most attentive to little Virginia, playing with her, bringing her small toys and trinkets. Several of the women have cooked meals and dropped them off with Mother to bring to Eleanor. At least she's eating.

The Indian women, in the fashion of the tribe, keened their mourning songs for Ananyas and Master Spendlove. Their voices echoed throughout the village. We wept to hear them; they wept to see us weeping. The bond between women is strong whenever there's a grievous loss.

I'm terribly worried about Eleanor, and so is Mother. She doesn't grieve the way she should, but prefers to stay secluded, seeing almost no one. I often wonder about the open manner in which the Indians express their sorrow; the women beat their breasts, the men cut their arms in mourning. Perhaps their way is better, for the grief is purged, mingling with tears and blood; then they can begin to heal.

"She's alone too much," Mother tells Father and he nods his head.

"What can we do?"

"Precious little," she replies, "but at least she finds comfort in Jess."

It's true. I sleep at night in her lodge house, listening to her smothered weeping. When I ask her if she wants me to leave, she grabs my hand and holds on for dear life.

"Stay with me," she entreats. "You're such a comfort."

I'm not sure how much comfort I really provide, but if she feels that way, so much the better.

But then Eleanor surprises us all, by leaving the cloistered dark of her lodge house and knocking on our door. It's early evening and we're just about to eat.

"Why, Eleanor," exclaims Mother, beckoning her to sit down. "Please join us."

Eleanor sits down, handing little Virginia to me. The babe smiles and begins playing with my hair.

"I have to go and find him... his body," she whispers in a trembling voice.

"Whatever do you mean?"

"I must go to his grave, find it. I must... see for myself...."

"That's ridiculous," Father interrupts. "Thomas Steueens wasn't even sure where they were when the hostiles attacked. It's much too dangerous."

Eleanor stares at him long and hard.

"I have to go," she repeats stubbornly. "For without knowing, I can have no peace."

Mother silences Father's argument with a flash of her eyes. I've seen that look she uses; Father knows it well. He stops speaking and begins eating his meal.

"What do you want to do that for?" Thomas asks.

"Sshh," Mother admonishes.

"Why, Thomas," Eleanor turns to him. "I must bring Ananyas back. We can have a Christian service for him here. We can consecrate the ground to make it... holy."

She closes her eyes. Father begins to cough and Mother frowns. She places her hand upon Eleanor's.

"We have no real church ground here."

"We can consecrate the earth by saying prayers. Surely that's possible?"

Mother's frown deepens.

"Eleanor, to leave this safe haven and venture into unknown wilderness... The same hostiles might be waiting...."

"Dear Mother Joyce, can't you see, I must bring Ananyas home. I can't eat, I can't sleep, until I know he's safe once more. There must be a place that I can bring my babe to see him, to offer prayers. Tell me you understand."

Mother's eyes brim with tears, as do mine. In my mind's eye, I picture little Virginia kneeling at her father's grave, wild flowers in her hand. My throat closes with the pain.

"Say that you'll help me in this quest. For if I don't find his grave and bring him home, then there's nothing...."

For the rest of the evening she sits quietly, eating but a little, watching me play with Virginia. Mother clears the supper table, then comes back to sit near Eleanor, reaching once more for her hand.

"Isn't it enough that prayers were said over his grave and that a cross stands to mark a man of Christ?"

Eleanor shakes her head. Her knuckles are white, gripping Mother's hand.

"Ananyas and I talked long into the night, before he left the next morning. He told me he'd come back. He promised me and my babe. It's only fitting that I help him keep his promise."

Mother weeps with Eleanor. Father gathers Thomas and the two of them go outside. I, alone, stay to rock Virginia in my arms. She's sleepy and her eyes begin to close. We sit there not saying a word, the only sound the muffled weeping, the catch in the throat. Finally, Eleanor gets up to leave.

"We'll keep Virginia here for the night," Mother offers.

"Oh, no," Eleanor replies, "for my babe is all I have left."

And she takes the sleeping child from my arms.

"You're such a good girl, Jess. What do you think?"

I glance at Mother, who shakes her head sorrowfully.

"It would be dangerous. And who knows where he lies. Perhaps you should wait...."

"I can't. Not until he's safe with me once more."

She leaves then, as silently as she came, the babe sound asleep in her arms. Mother comes and sits by my side.

"I understand how she feels," I say to her. "I surely do. Is it possible...?"

"No," she answers sadly. "For we're safe only here, with the Croatoans... your friends... and mine."

Chapter 10

Eleanor's Idea

I ENTER ELEANOR'S LODGE house to see her chopping viciously at her beautiful long hair.

"What are you doing?"

"I'm cutting it. Then I'll mix a dye and change its color. I'll dress in buckskin and go myself. I'll look like a man...."

"You can't," I gasp. "You can't possibly go yourself. You don't even know where to begin."

"It doesn't matter."

"And how will you bring his body back, even if you should be lucky enough to find his grave?"

She shakes her head.

"Our Good Lord will help me. He'll direct my path. Will you keep my secret?"

I nod my head mutely, for I am mesmerized by the raw intensity of her voice, her actions. When at last her beautiful long hair lies in clumps upon the floor, she stares at herself in the long-handled mirror she's kept safe all the way from England.

"I look awful," she cries and bursts into tears. She turns to me.

"Will you come with me? And Akaiyan? You said he's traveled north before. Skotai can give him directions."

I sit there dumb-founded. For what she's proposing is foolhardy and dangerous. But, surprising even myself, I nod my head for I know how much she loved, still loves, Ananyas.

She's stopped before she can even gather up the fallen clumps of hair. Mother and Father come into the room and Mother, seeing what she's done, bursts into tears and throws her arms about Eleanor. They cry together.

"I forbid it," Father says firmly. "You must put such thoughts out of your head."

There's much sobbing. Mother takes Eleanor and Virginia to our house, while I'm left to sweep the floor and gather Eleanor's shorn locks into a pile. Rather than throw them away, I wrap them in a cloth and tuck them under her pillow. Then I run after them both.

The whole village speaks of nothing else. The men and women shake their heads at her foolishness. The Indians stare at her short-cropped hair peeking out beneath her bonnet. Eleanor walks about with her lips set grimly. Her face grows even more gaunt.

"Could we find Ananyas's grave?"

I'm sitting with Akaiyan, watching him clean a rabbit. He's gutted the entrails and is now skinning it. What a messy job, but I'm not bothered watching. He's even taught me to clean fish the *unqua* way, a task I used to hate.

He stares at me, his deep brown eyes searching mine. I stare back at him .

"Could we?"

"Skotai has told me the place. My father and I passed

through there on our journey north. It is not near any *unqua* camp. The ones who attacked them must have been a far-ranging raiding party."

"Could we?" I ask again.

He shakes his head.

"I know what you are thinking, Little Bird. But it would be a long and dangerous journey. You could not come."

"Why not?"

"It is far away from the shoreline, from this place."

"*Untateawa?*"

"Far," he repeats. "Deep in the woodlands. My father would never allow it."

I think of Manteo.

"We needn't tell him," I answer boldly. Akaiyan stares at me.

"Eleanor can't go. She has her babe. She couldn't leave Virginia. I think she wants us, me and you, to go in her place."

He shakes his head again and gets up, his hands bloody from the rabbit.

"I go to wash."

"Think about it," I run after him. "I want to go."

"But why?"

"Because it's only fitting that we bring Ananyas home. No one else will do it. And if we can't bring his body back, then I can say the prayers she wants to say. I can say them in English and in Croatoan. I'm already more *unqua* than anyone. I'll cut my hair like Eleanor did. I'm not afraid...."

Akaiyan grunts. Then he reaches out to touch my cheek.

"Little Bird, you are indeed like the *unqua*. Does this mean so much to you?"

"If you don't go, then... then, I'll go myself...."

He throws back his head and laughs softly.

"I will talk to Skotai," he says then.

"*Kawa?*"

"*Kawa.*"

Oh, I'm full of trepidation. How can I have suggested such a thing? Mother and Father will never allow it. But how can I not go? Eleanor weeps all day and through the long night. She grows thinner and thinner. Not one of our brave settlers will venture forth on her behalf. I loved Ananyas, too, remembering how he always spoke so kindly to me and Thomas, how he took my side in so many ways. He should be brought home for this is, indeed, our home now. He must rest in consecrated ground. I run behind Akaiyan, who turns when he hears me. Without shame, I kiss him gently on the cheek.

"*Unta hah?*"

"Yes," he answers slowly, putting my hand to his lips. "I will go along with you."

Chapter 11

Secret Preparations

TWO DAYS LATER, Akaiyan tells me that Skotai will come with us also, to point the way to where Ananyas and Master Spendlove are buried.

I tell no one. Mother and Father will be furiously angry with me for even thinking such thoughts. But this is something I feel I must do, for Eleanor's sake, for Ananyas's soul. I feel Eleanor's pain so deeply. There'll be no respite for her until Ananyas is buried in consecrated ground near the village. Only then will she be able to begin the healing process.

My heart beats fast whenever I think of leaving. It will certainly be a long and dangerous journey. What will Mother do when she finds I'm gone? What will Father say? I know this will hurt them terribly, but I'm committed now and there's no turning back.

Akaiyan has gathered some simple supplies. Like Ananyas and those who left with him, we plan to live off the land. I'm not afraid to sleep upon leaves in the forest, not as long as Akaiyan is with me. I trust him completely to watch over me, for didn't he say long ago, "Little Bird, Akaiyan will take care of you?"

But I've packed a cover to protect us all, some clothing, a few sheets of paper, my pen, of course, and cloths to wrap Ananyas's body in when we find it. I'll leave that most unpleasant task to Akaiyan. I've also decided to confide in Eleanor, pledging her to secrecy on my behalf.

"You can't go!" she exclaims at first. "It's much too dangerous!"

"I must," I answer. "For you'll sicken if you don't find peace."

She begins to weep quietly. Then she gently places her Holy Bible in my hands.

"If you can't bring him back, read these passages over his grave. I've marked them off. And dig a hole and bury this near his heart."

She tugs at her wedding ring, handing it to me.

"You mustn't give me this."

"Why not? It does me no good anymore. Place it near my beloved Ananyas's heart, for we're joined for all eternity."

I take her silver band and place it upon my finger. It gleams in the sunlight. Eleanor gives me a kiss.

"I'll pray every day and night for your safe return." She pauses. "I have a special secret. Even now, as we speak, new life stirs within my womb. Oh, my poor Ananyas! He won't see his child born. And your dear Mother. What shall I tell her?"

I don't know how to answer, for Mother will be distraught, I know. She'll want to send the men to bring us back.

"We're leaving after everyone's asleep. This way, we'll have a good head start. Don't let Father come after us. You'll have to think of something."

But she's weeping again and doesn't reply. I give her a quick hug, leaning my head upon her shoulder. Eleanor's been more a sister to me than if I had one. For one brief moment, doubts come crowding into my head. I steel my back and turn to go.

"If we can find him, we'll bring him home, I promise."

She stares at me, her eyes red from weeping.

"Yes," she says then, "bring him home."

And so, that every evening after everyone's asleep, I gather myself from my warm bed and meet Akaiyan and Skotai outside. There are no words exchanged between us, just a quick nod of the head, then off we run into the woods. My heart aches to leave my dear mother and father sleeping so trustingly. And Thomas, my brother, surely I'll miss him as well. For a moment I hesitate, stopping to turn and glance back at Akaiyan's village, my village now. The smoke from the smoldering fires wafts slowly toward the skies. The stars shine brightly in the firmament, the moon is half-full. A wolf howls in the far distance, then falls silent again.

"Quickly," Akaiyan whispers and we run down to the far beach, there to take a canoe and row across the narrow strip of water to the land I've called in the past, "the skinny finger of God." It stretches between us and the cold, forbidding outer sea, both protecting and luring us on with its mystery. From there, we'll go north, ever north toward our destiny, crossing whatever waters we encounter with the canoe carried upon Akaiyan's and Skotai's shoulders.

We run at a steady pace, though Akaiyan watches to make sure I don't fall behind. I know he's concerned and worried about my coming along. But surely he knows also that I have no choice, driven as I am by the passion of my heart!

Chapter 12

Heading North

WE'VE BEEN GONE NOW ten whole days. I was sure in the beginning that I'd see Father and some of the other men running through the woods behind us. But there's not been a sound except our own footfalls, as we move carefully through the woodlands.

Akaiyan has been most cautious, on many occasions sending Skotai to scout ahead. Then he, too, takes his turn. This way, if there's danger, only one will be caught by surprise. But it's been raining for most of the time and this, Akaiyan says, is good. It covers our sounds, and it keeps any hunting parties in their camp. I always disliked the rain, especially when it rained incessantly as we sailed across the mighty sea on our good ship, The Red Lyon. But now, I kneel and give thanks to our Lord and Savior, Jesus Christ, and to Akaiyan's Great Spirit, for the sweet and protective rainfall.

I've learned why the Indians use buckskin for their clothing. The water runs off the *ocques* we're wearing, keeping us dry and warm underneath. Only my hair is wet, but it dries quickly whenever the sun appears from behind the clouds. For it was cut, as Eleanor had cut hers, that early morn after we crept away. Akaiyan took his razor-sharp knife and cut, not in a straight line as a scissors would have done, but in the way that feathers of a bird lie against its body, overlapping each other. I'm rather pleased with the way I now look; it's short like a boy's, but not unattractive. Akaiyan kept muttering as he used his knife. I know it pained him to have to cut my long hair. But it's easier to look after and safer....

He also stained my skin with the berries Skotai gathered. The parts of my body which show, my hands and arms and face, are no longer white but brown like his. My hair is stained dark as well. I hardly recognize myself, and tell Akaiyan that it's like camouflage, though there's no word in Croatoan that means exactly that.

We travel as far as we can each day, catching only a few hours of sleep at night. We get up before the sunrise and move on. Akaiyan and Skotai are both good hunters. They've caught rabbits and squirrels. We make only small fires, lighting them barely long enough to roast the meat, using fatwood sticks dried by the heat of their bodies as they run. Sometimes the wood is too wet and both Akaiyan and Skotai eat the meat raw. I've yet to try a piece of uncooked rabbit, preferring those times to eat the berries and nuts they've gathered.

And so we go on, heading ever north. We've left the narrow strip of land, crossing a slim channel and are on the mainland now. I can no longer see the sea in the distance, even when I strain my eyes, nor hear the breakers which echoed in our ears.

The trees grow thickly around us and the going is sometimes hard. Akaiyan says that this is also in our favor, for the trees offer protection from the rain and from any hostiles. But we've yet to see a single sign of a hunting party and I'm greatly relieved.

The canoe is heavy for them to carry, and Akaiyan talks long with Skotai about leaving it behind, covered with soft pine branches.

"What happens if we come to more *awoo?*" I ask.

"We'll cross the big water in a raft I shall build," he replies.

I have great respect for the skill of the *unqua*. Making a raft is certainly easier than crafting a canoe, but trees must be felled and this isn't easy. I watched once when the men selected a cypress tree for one of their *ooshunnawa*. They set small fires all around its base, keeping them burning low and steadily. When the trunk was charred through, the big tree toppled easily. Then they stripped off its branches and leaves, hollowing out the inside as best they could, often smearing pitch and resin and lighting small fires which burned and charred the wood so they could continue scraping. It was a long and tedious process but when finished, the hollowed-out trunk was wide enough within for a man to sit. The *unqua* also have an interesting habit of hiding their *ooshunnawa* by sinking them in shallow streams. There they rest, safe from enemies, until needed.

Akaiyan and Skotai decide to hide the canoe, noting where we can retrieve it when we pass this way again. There is no stream in which to sink it, so Skotai cuts many branches, draping them artfully over the canoe until even I can't see it.

There are many nights I'm cold, even wrapped snugly in my covering. I shiver and try to sleep, listening to the sounds of *untuch* falling, and *hoonoch* blowing through the trees. Akaiyan comes over.

"You are cold?" he questions.

I nod my head, trying not to shiver in front of him.

"I could use an *oowaiana,* for then I could boil some water to make tea."

I can almost taste Mistress Steueens sweet honey brew. He sits down next to me, putting his arm about my shoulders. It's the first time he's touched me in such a manner.

"I should not have brought you," he says, shaking his head again. "Skotai and I could find the grave."

"No, I had to come. If we can't bring him back, then I need to say special prayers over his body. Eleanor gave me her wedding band to leave there."

I show him the silver ring. He nods his head.

"My father's wife, his *kateocca,* my mother, died when my brother was born. My father grieved for a very long time. We sang the mourning songs and performed many rituals, but the sadness was deep within him. It took many moons to lessen his grief. Often I could hear him weep during *oosottoo* when the winds blew hard and snow fell, and he thought we were all sleeping."

I lean against his warm chest.

"Eleanor weeps at night, all night long. She can't rest until we bring Ananyas home."

"To the land far across the sea?"

"No," I say, "to our home... with you and your people... my home."

Chapter 13

Unknown Graves

THE PATTERN OF OUR LIVES seems set. We rest during the day, traveling mainly at night. This way, Akaiyan says, we will avoid any hunting parties. It's hard to sleep when the sun shines brightly overhead, and even scarier to move at night, when the animals howl and the noises are strange and unfamiliar.

Several times, I trip over tree roots and small stones until, at last, Akaiyan holds my hand to steady me. Skotai is always in the forefront, leading the way. He's older than Akaiyan, but not as old as Manteo. Nor is he as handsome as either, for his nose is crooked, once broken in a fight with a bear. There's a scar down his right cheek left by that same bear, and one on his chest from the raking claws. But around his neck he wears those claws and also, its teeth, a sign of his triumph. In his lodge house at home is the *oochehara*, bearskin, to keep him warm during the winter nights.

The way is not direct. Skotai leads us on a winding path,

heading east, heading west. Sometimes I think he doesn't remember where Ananyas lies, though Akaiyan says he does. The zig-zag route we take is to cover our tracks and avoid the hostiles and any Spanish.

I hadn't thought at all about the Spanish who might be lurking in these woods. The Spaniards supposedly based their explorations much further south, in a place they called Florida. But then I remember Father saying that they, too, sought the Chesapeake lands, calling them the *Bahía de Santa Maria*. What if we find them when we finally reach our destination? What if they've taken over the encampment of our brave colonists who sailed away that sad November day? Where would George Howe be now, or Dyonis and Margaret Harvye and their babe? Such black thoughts consume me that, on occasion, I can barely breathe. It's then that Akaiyan signals Skotai to stop and we rest, so I can catch my breath or else, weep quietly in Akaiyan's arms. I'm certain neither he nor Skotai understand such emotion. The *unqua*, I've learned, are a quiet people and quite stoic in their ways. So attuned to nature, they seem to accept hardships much more easily than the *nickreruroh*, Englishmen.

But Akaiyan is patient with me, allowing me to rest and gather my thoughts, holding me when I cry. I don't think he was bonded to anyone in his tribe before he met me. The ties between us grow stronger each day.

On our twelfth day, we stop to rest as dawn reddens the sky. Grateful to ease the cramp in my legs, I sink down upon the earthen floor of the forest. Akaiyan searches for rabbit while Skotai remains ever vigilant, watching the trees and deeper woods for any sign of movement. All of a sudden, I feel a slithering motion by my legs and I scream.

"What is it?"

Akaiyan comes running. Trembling all over, I point to a large snake which I'd disturbed. It slithers away but Akaiyan is too fast. He laughs, picking it up just behind its head where it can't bite him.

"Kill it, oh, kill it!"

"Why should I kill it? For it has not harmed you. We treat the *us-quauh-ne* with respect. If we do not bother him, he will not bother us."

To please me, Akaiyan takes the snake to a distant place. He smiles as he comes back.

"You are not yet *unqua*, Little Bird, only part *unqua*."

I make a face, then am instantly sorry.

After we've slept for most of the day, hidden by a small outcrop of rocks, we eat and start on the night's sojourn. The moon is full, bathing the woods in silver. We half-walk, half-jog for a while, then come to a small clearing. Skotai points and both Akaiyan and I see some crosses set in the ground.

"Is this where Ananyas lies?"

Skotai shakes his head.

"Not *nickreruroh*," says Akaiyan. He mutters the word for Spanish.

"This is not a good place," he pulls on my hand. "Come away."

But I must see for myself. I drag him reluctantly to the crosses. There are three of them, set unevenly about the clearing. Now that I'm closer, I can see the mounded earth beneath them, each harboring a body. I shudder.

"Are you sure these are Spanish...?" I start to ask, then read the crude lettering on each cross. I can't read my enemy's language, but I can ascertain the names: Alonso de Velasco, Domingo de Mendoza, Lucas Méndez Canzo. What strange-sounding names!

"Come," Akaiyan insists, pulling me roughly away.

"But why would they be buried here?" I wonder out loud.

"Killed by Weapemeoc. We must go."

I stumble into the woods after Akaiyan, my heart full of dread. For the Spanish, my enemy, have buried three of their dead, placing them in shallow graves as Ananyas and Master Spendlove were placed. As my mother once cried out to me long ago, we are all vulnerable in this wild, inhospitable land. And death honors no man above another!

Chapter 14

Captured

LAST NIGHT, I HEARD howling and awoke with a start to see yellow eyes gleaming through the trees.

"Akaiyan," I called urgently. "The wolves are here."

He was by my side in a flash.

"One *squarrena*," he said. "And an old one. He hunts alone, banished forever from his pack."

He threw a stone in the wolf's direction. The eyes disappeared into the trees.

"Maybe he'll come back?"

"No, Little Bird. He's *werricauna* now. But I shall sit with you so you can sleep."

Once more, he put his arm about my shoulders. I leaned sleepily against him.

"Will you be banished from your pack, for taking me with you?"

He sighed.

"My father is a... strict man. He will be *cotcheroore*, angry for my arrogance."

"What do you mean, arrogance?"

"To take a *nickreruroh* into the unknown lands."

"I'm not a *nickreruroh*, I'm an *unqua*. No matter what you say, I'm more of an *unqua* than most!"

Akaiyan bent his head suddenly and placed his lips upon mine. His kiss was like goose down, light, but soft and warm.

"Oh," I gasped, then without more thinking, kissed him back most passionately. We clung to each other for a few moments, then he pulled away.

"To kiss you brings me much joy," he whispered. "Is this what English do?"

"When they love someone," I answered softly.

"Perhaps I love you," he said, then got up abruptly and went back to his sleeping place. I stayed awake for the rest of the night.

Three more days pass as we travel higher up the mainland. I try to remember the route Ananyas had sketched, based on John White's maps, for he'd let us all see his path to the Chesapeake. We're not heading away from the sea, as I'd originally thought. Going up those outer banks of land, instead of rowing across and past Roanoak, has kept us roughly parallel to the water. If I recall Ananyas's map, we're headed directly for the Chesapeake, with many miles still to go.

When Akaiyan finally signals us to rest, I write a brief letter to my mother. If anything should happen to me, then she'll know my innermost thoughts.

Dearest Mother,

It's my most fervent wish that you'll forgive me for leaving you and Father. I've gone with Akaiyan and Skotai to search out Ananyas's grave and bring him home. If that's possible,

then you'll see us soon enough, for Skotai seems to feel we're
close to the site. If we can't find the grave, or if it's impossible
to bring his body home, then I shall say many prayers where
he lies. Eleanor has given me her silver wedding band to bury,
should the latter happen. Please, dearest Mother, don't be
angry with me. In my heart, I feel I'm doing the right thing.
You needn't worry, Akaiyan is taking good care of me. With
love, your devoted daughter.

I fold the paper and carefully place it with Eleanor's ring,
in the amulet pouch I wear around my neck, hidden inside
my bodice.

"Over there," Skotai whispers, pointing to a grove of
trees. I can see two crosses in the distance, so I run quickly.
Akaiyan shouts for me to wait, but I can't. Dear Ananyas, I'm
so close, soon, soon, you'll be in hallowed ground on Croatoan
Island. Eleanor's tears shall wash away your pain and cleanse
your spirit, freeing it up to Heaven. You'll never be alone
again.

"*¡Mira lo que acabo de agarrar!*"

Rough hands reach out to grab me and tighten around
my waist. A hand is clamped over my mouth. I try to scream
but can't. I can smell the sweat, see the shine of... Spanish
armor.

Another voice calls out,
"*Tráelo aquí.*"
I hear a third voice shouting,
"*¡Hay dos más!*"
Akaiyan is calling, calling, then I swoon....

Chapter 15

Imprisoned

IT'S DARK WHEN I AWAKE, my joints aching. For several minutes I can't see a thing. Then my eyes adjust to the dim light. No wonder I can't move; my hands are bound behind me, as well as my legs. I'm confined in some small space which smells musty and damp. I can sense movement, the tilt and roll of something upon the water. Surely, I must be on a ship!

Panic overwhelms me in waves. I gulp to fight back the nausea which threatens. Where am I? Then I remember, a low moan escaping my lips. I've been caught by Spanish soldiers. I can hear the shouts far above me in the language of my enemies.

I'm left there for at least two hours, feeling the roll and pitch of the large vessel. Oh, where is Akaiyan? Where is Skotai? What will my father think now?

I must have somehow fallen asleep, for when I awaken once more, it's lighter. A small porthole up near the beamed ceiling lets sun in. I'm in some sort of rough cabin, with just a bench and a table. My buckskin top is flecked with spots of dried blood, whose? Then the memory comes flooding back. I bit one Spaniard's hand, drawing blood and angry cries. He must have slapped me, for my cheek is swollen.

Akaiyan lies in the corner, hands and feet tightly bound. He's still unconscious. Maybe he's dead! I've no way of knowing until I see the faint rise and fall of his chest, and I breathe a sigh of relief. So he's still alive. There's no sign of Skotai and I wonder if he escaped.

My tunic top is not only blood-flecked but slightly torn. I wonder if Spanish hands were upon me, shuddering with this terrible thought. I must free myself and go to Akaiyan. Together, we may yet be able to escape.

But where would we go? For if we're on a Spanish ship, then we're upon the sea. I can smell the salt air and feel the ship's keel as it cuts the water deep.

"Akaiyan," I call urgently, hoping he'll hear me. He moans and stirs.

"Oh, Akaiyan, please, please wake up. It's me, Jess, Little Bird...."

He struggles to a sitting position. His mouth is swollen from several blows and he's bleeding from a cut above his eye.

"Skotai?" he whispers hoarsely, looking around. When he sees me, he groans.

"Akaiyan, where's Skotai? What's happened?"

"Little Bird, *oonutsauka*, I remember, the men in metal have caught us. Skotai was shot by one of their soldiers. I would have killed him, but I was clubbed...."

"Can you free your hands?"

He rubs and rubs his wrists against the wall until he's bleeding, but the bonds are tight. We sit there staring at each

other, listening to the cries above us. Akaiyan sees my torn bodice.

"If they touched you, I will... kill them. I will...."

I jump as the cabin door is pushed open. Rough soldiers come in and pull both me and Akaiyan to a standing position. They cut the ties on our arms and legs and push us forward.

"*Vamos, vamos,*" they gesture, pointing ahead. We leave the cabin and are brought on deck. There, in front of all the enemy, we are forced to stand until their captain comes.

"*Los indios,*" he says in a gutteral voice.

I want to say that I'm English, but something in his voice tells me I'm better off pretending to be an Indian. I glare defiantly, holding my head high, though inside I am weak and terribly afraid.

"No," he says then in broken English. "Not *los indios. ¿Tú eres inglés...?*"

I shake my head savagely.

He turns to Akaiyan and smacks him sharply across the face.

"*El Indio,* you... but... not him... *Yo reconozco a un inglés cuando yo veo a uno.*"

After that, everything is a blur. Akaiyan is prodded back down the rough steps and I'm led to the upper deck. The captain points to me and pulls at his beard.

"*Inglés...,*" he says, leaning his face close to mine. "*¿Por qué estás vestido como un indio?*"

I'm trembling all over. If I don't sit down soon, I'll fall....

He peers at me again.

"*¿Por qué?*"

I shrug my shoulders, then I give a sudden gasp. He has slapped me across my face. Oh, I mustn't cry in front of him.

"*¿Qué pasa?*"

And then I realize he's not sure if I'm English. Nor does he have any idea where we come from. I must lead them away from thoughts of Roanoak and Croatoan Islands. Without speaking, I point toward the west.

"*Unqua*," I say in as deep a voice as I can. "*Ut chat.*"

I'm sure he doesn't understand, so I point again to the west with my arm outstretched. He can see that I won't say anymore. For a moment, I think that he might hit me again, but he doesn't.

"Aah," he says finally, nodding his head and looking across the deck to the blurred ridge of coastline in the distance. He snaps an order to a seaman, and I'm led down below and pushed once more into that small room. Akaiyan is gone.

"Akaiyan," I call out, beating my fists against the locked cabin door. "Akaiyan, Akaiyan!"

But no one answers and I'm alone.

Chapter 16

The Secret

ONCE MORE, I'M LEFT ALONE for several hours. My cheek hurts where the captain hit me. However, my hands and feet haven't been bound again, so I'm free to explore my surroundings. Apart from the slight tear in my buckskin top, there are no other signs of assault on me. I kneel and give thanks to God that, so far, they think me a *wariaugh,* a boy. I give thanks for my slender build and my close-cropped dyed hair.

But where is Akaiyan? Why have they separated us? Has he been killed and, even now, thrown overboard to feed the *cunshe*? And more puzzling, why didn't they kill us when they first caught us? These, and a hundred other thoughts, whirl around in my head.

I hear a key turning in the lock and see the door opening. Immediately, I back against the far wall, keeping my eyes lowered. A young soldier comes in, no older, I think, than seventeen. He brings food in a plate.

"*¡Come!*" he says, thrusting the plate at me.

I take it gratefully for, no matter what, I must eat to keep up my strength.

"*Indio,*" he keeps saying over and over, and I realize it's possible he's never seen an Indian up close before.

"Akaiyan?" I ask, keeping my voice as deep as possible. "*Caunotka,* brother? *Kahunk,* now!"

He gestures helplessly at me, because he doesn't understand. I point to the corner where Akaiyan was.

"Akaiyan? Akaiyan?"

"*Si,*" he says then, realizing what I want. "*El indio está fuera de peligro.*"

¿Fuera de peligro? What can that mean? Is Akaiyan dead or is he safe somewhere? I nod my head and give a smile.

"*¿Fuera de peligro?*"

"*Sí, él está bien.*"

I take a chance that he's telling me Akaiyan is all right.

"Where?" I ask excitedly, then realize my mistake. His eyes widen and he stares at me.

"*¿Inglés...?*"

I put a finger to my lips, shaking my head.

"*Por favor, no, indio, indio....*"

My fate lies in this young soldier's hands as he backs away. He's too scared, and I'm so frightened that he'll tell his captain.

"*Por favor,*" I plead again, walking toward him. "*Indio, por favor.*"

For a moment, time stops. There's nothing but the creak and groan of this Spanish ship, the slap of the water against the hull. Even the cries of the sailors are nothing, nothing. We're alone, he and I, in an unknown wilderness. What will he do? What will he do? I stare at him and he stares back. We're so close I can see the tiny beads of sweat on his forehead, the sprouting of a young man's moustache upon his upper lip. A soldier's uniform but a boy's eyes. He could be another George Howe. A little sigh of breath escapes me. He hears it and gives the faintest of smiles. It's then that I know God is surely with me, for he puts a finger to his lips.

"*Sí*," he whispers, "*indio*."

It's all I can do not to run and hug him. He backs up toward the door. At the last minute, he turns, "*Yo puedo guardar un secreto*," then leaves, closing and locking the door behind him. My heart is racing and I can hardly breathe. Time passes slowly. I strain to hear the sound of boots on the rough planking telling me that they're coming for me, that the young Spanish soldier has betrayed my secret to his captain. And am I worse off pretending to be an Indian? What do the Spanish do to Indians? I've no way of knowing.

Chapter 17

Can We Escape?

FOR MOST OF THE DAY, I've been left alone to sit and ponder my situation. I've eaten the food the young soldier brought me. It isn't very good, mainly cold rice, a few beans and something that could have been meat but is full of gristle. I haven't eaten that. I need a drink right now, for my lips are dry and cracking. I hope he comes back soon with water.

There's no place to go to the bathroom other than an old, rusted bucket in one corner. If I were truly a boy, it wouldn't be a problem. However, I manage as best I can, praying fervently that no one unlocks the door and enters while I'm ministering to myself.

The hours pass slowly. The only way I can tell time is by the small light filtering through the porthole above. The room is mainly dark, no matter what. I'm glad they've left me unbound, for I have freedom to move and stretch my legs. I'm in one piece, unharmed so far except for my slightly swollen cheek. I wonder what my fate will be.

Just thinking such thoughts makes me want to weep. What of my poor mother and father back on Croatoan Island? What must they be feeling? How foolish I was to think I could venture into the wilderness, find Ananyas's grave and bring his body back. I'm being punished for my arrogant ways. This is a lesson God is teaching me, to be humbled so I can repent.

But forgive me, sweet Lord, for this arrogance which still lurks in a small corner of my mind. For was I not trying to ease Eleanor's grief and pain? Surely it would have been more sinful to do nothing? I'm wracked with such confusing thoughts.

The soldiers come once more and lead me above. I'm relieved to breathe in sweet, fresh air, but full of trepidation. This Spanish captain is an unknown factor, and that scares me. What has he done with Akaiyan? What does he plan to do with me?

"*Indio*," he says, once more pulling on his thick black beard. His teeth are yellowed. "*Mi nombre es Vicente González. ¿Has oído de mí?*"

Though inwardly I gasp, remembering the stories of Vicente González, this Spanish brigand, from Father and the others, I try to keep my face unmoved. I shrug my shoulders and say in Croatoan,

"Where is my *caunotka*, brother, Akaiyan?"

He gives a hearty laugh and spouts rapid-fire Spanish to his men, who laugh also. I can't understand a word.

"*Indio*," and he peers closely at me, "that *indio*, Ak..Ak...kayanno... ¿es él tu hermano...? Your... brother...?"

He pulls Akaiyan from behind the mast post. My heart leaps in my throat, for they haven't killed him. His hands are tied and his head down. Have they beaten him?

"*Los indios traerán buen dinero cuando sean vendidos como esclavos.*"

Though I can't understand the Spanish words, his intention becomes clear. The only reason they haven't killed us is because they have plans to sell us into slavery. I stand there defiantly.

"Bring *agua,*" he says, and I'm handed a ladle of cold water. I drink it gratefully. Vicente González doesn't want his captives to die before their time.

They tie me with *utsera,* rope, to the mast next to Akaiyan. For a moment no words are exchanged between us, for the Spaniards who are nearby watch us with curiosity. But then their duties call them to different parts of the ship, and we're briefly alone.

"Akaiyan," I whisper in Croatoan, "are you well?"

He nods his head and whispers back.

"They must not think you *nickreruroh.* They must not think you *con-noowa,* woman."

"I know. They think I'm *unqua,* a *wariaugh.* I've told them you're *caunotka.*"

We whisper back and forth as much as we dare. The Spanish ship moves heavily through the waters, not at all like our English ones. It's a cumbersome vessel, pushing the waves roughly aside with its blunt-nosed prow. I glance up to see seagulls flying about the mast.

"We're coming to some land," I tell Akaiyan excitedly. "There we can escape."

He raises his head and I see his swollen, bloodied lips, his battered face. He speaks haltingly.

"*Oousotto,* yesterday, I thought I would die. *Kawa,* I live because you are here with me. Little Bird, I... love you, like the English say."

My eyes fill with tears.

"*Jureha, jureha,* if we anchor, we'll get free from these

Spanish rogues. We'll find a way to run into the woods."

He stares at me with eyes deep like the pools of night, and I stare back at him, bound for all eternity to his heart.

"*Unta hah?*" and he nods his head.

Chapter 18

The Spanish Garrison

THE NEXT MORNING when I awake, I find myself alone in the small cabin which has been my prison. I've not been harmed and there's fresh food on the plate near me. I can sense that the ship is no longer plowing roughly through the waters but is anchored, the rasp of the heavy metal chain rubbing against its hull. What have they done with Akaiyan?

The door opens and the young soldier comes in. He brings a metal cup full of sweet water, and holds it out to me. Glancing at the uneaten food, he speaks in words I can't understand,

"¿Come?"

When I don't answer, he pretends to eat, picking up imaginary food and putting his fingers to his mouth.

"¿Inglés...?"

"Indio, indio," I repeat stubbornly, but feel strangely disquieted. Has he told anyone?

"Inglés," and he stands there staring.

I'm trembling all over, hardly able to stand, for he must have told his captain. I keep shaking my head.

To my great distress, a single tear runs down my cheek. I wipe it away with haste, the young soldier watching curiously. He moves closer. With a sudden movement, too quick for me to stop him, he places his hand lightly upon my bodice, feeling the slight swell of my breasts hidden beneath the buckskin. His eyes widen even further.

"*¡Tú eres una chica!*"

I pull away from him, but he doesn't follow. Now it will happen, I think in great panic, all those terrible stories of rape will come true. But still he stands there, his hand outstretched, a look of puzzlement upon his face. Were it not for the Spanish uniform, he could be just a boy from any English country town. Why doesn't he sound alarm? Why doesn't he try to take advantage of me? He shakes his head then, and slowly picks up the plate from the wooden table. I reach into my bodice and pull out the amulet pouch containing my letter and Eleanor's silver wedding band. Quickly, I take the ring and hand it to him. He rolls it back and forth between his fingers.

"Take it," I say in English. "Take it, *por favor*, but only keep my secret."

"*¿Secreto?*"

"Yes," nodding my head. "*Unqua, wariaugh.* I'm an Indian, a boy," in English for emphasis.

Suddenly, there's nothing left to do but kneel down upon the hard planking and put my hands together in fervent prayer.

"Dear Heavenly Father, sweet Jesus, I pray for my safety and that of Akaiyan."

"*Jesús,*" he whispers and quickly crosses himself.

"*Jesús, Dios Mío.*" Then he leaves quietly without saying another word. I'm left breathless and full of fear.

We're taken off the ship, Akaiyan and I, our hands bound tightly once more. The Spanish soldiers watch with great interest. There's no chance to talk, for the air is full of bustling sounds. We're rowed to shore where there appears to be a small encampment. I've never seen so many Spaniards, more than *nauocq*, fleas, on a dog. Unlike our original settlement on Roanoak, this is a military garrison. From what I can understand, we've arrived at their *Bahía de Santa Maria*, our Chesapeake. The ship has anchored within a large body of water, high in the northern part of the Baye. But it makes no sense, for there are no signs of any English around. On one side, the land juts like a promontory into a large sea, so wide and distant that I can't see its other sides.

The young soldier is in the boat that puts us to shore. His eyes are upon me at all times and I try not to look at him. I'm more concerned with Akaiyan, for he has been newly beaten; there's fresh blood on his back.

"Did they whip you?" I whisper.

"With a *chinqua*, stick," he answers.

I glare defiantly at the young soldier. His people are a brutal race of men, to beat a person whose hands are bound. What will be our fate when we land in this accursed place? I haven't stopped trembling.

Once on land, they tie us to a post in the center of the garrison for all to see. Vicente González engages in much talk with the Spanish captain in charge, exchanging documents and some trinkets. The captain points to us and gestures. He hands González some gold and silver coins. González speaks to him and they both laugh and go inside one of the rough huts.

71

We're forced to stand all afternoon tied to the post like two of their dogs. At dusk, the young soldier comes with another, not much older, and unties us. They lead Akaiyan and me to a hut where we're put inside. Water and food is brought. My hands are left untied, but not Akaiyan's. The young Spanish soldier claps the other on the back and they both leave. He glances back at me before closing and locking the door behind him.

"We must escape," I tell Akaiyan. He nods his head. I make him drink some water and eat some of the food. It has maggots in it.

We spend a restless night, listening to the strange Spanish sounds echoing outside, the coarse laughter, the moan of the wind rising in the trees. I manage to curl up next to Akaiyan, grateful for his body warmth.

"Little Bird," he says sorrowfully, "I have never been *werricauna* before, but...."

"Sshh," I say, putting my finger on his cracked lips, "*tnotsaurauweek*, don't speak of it any more."

Chapter 19

Los Esclavos

I'VE LEARNED WELL what Vicente González meant when he spoke of *los esclavos*. We have been sold as slaves, Akaiyan and I, slaves to the soldiers of that garrison. Akaiyan works for the captain, a brute of a man called Pedro de Avilés. I have been assigned to a lower rank soldier, one named Antonio Cabeza de Vaca. The captain paid González many coins of silver and gold for us.

It seems that we're lucky not to have been killed. But slavery is a fate worse than death, I believe. We work from sunrise to sunset, fetching water, fetching wood, currying their *a hots,* which I know as horses, but which Akaiyan has never seen before. I'd heard that the Spanish always brought their horses with them. It's hard to imagine these gentle animals crowded together in a small, dark hold, with little air and no fresh hay to eat. How could such cargo be transported across the vast western ocean in the belly of a ship?

These horses have thick legs and solid backs, sturdy

73

beasts strong enough to carry a man in full armor. There are only six of them left, for several died on the Spanish ship during one fearsome storm. They have big velvet eyes and soft brown skin, which glistens after a good brushing. I like working with the *a hots*, for their ways are gentle and *uisau-wanne*, soft. They whinny whenever Akaiyan and I come near and yesterday, the brown mare who is heavy with foal leaned her head against my shoulder, blowing her warm breath in my face.

Akaiyan was afraid at first, thinking they were some sort of monster. But then he grew used to them, and they to him. When he sees the soldiers mount their backs, or watches them pull a cart, he marvels at their strength, equally fascinated and *werricauna* at the same time. I've whispered to him that the English have these horses back home, bigger and stronger, but he simply asks, why didn't we bring them with us? I don't know the answer.

The *capitán*, as he's called, orders Akaiyan about imperiously, often kicking him whenever he goes by. I'm more fortunate in that respect. Antonio Cabeza de Vaca is less concerned with beating me than seeing that I have his armor shined, his boots spotless. He barely says a word to me and I'm careful never to slip into the English tongue. There's no need, for the only one I care to converse with is Akaiyan, and we speak Croatoan whenever we get the chance. This happens only at night, for when he's grooming the horses, I'm scrubbing thick mud off boots, or sweeping a dirt hut.

It seems we're a novelty to these Spaniards, two Indian brothers captured together. The soldiers often gawk at us while we work; it makes me most uncomfortable. At *oosottoo*, when every one's sleeping, I lie awake thinking of ways we can possibly escape. But each sunset, a chain is linked around

our ankles, and Akaiyan and I are locked in a hut together. All we can do is dream.

I'm worried that the young soldier who first brought me food and drink will betray my secret. I rarely see him, for he's at work with others making their ship ready to sail again. I believe they're bound for Spain. Vicente González carries much gold and silver as his cargo, for I've managed to learn some of the Spanish words and keep my ears open for any scrap of news.

I dream constantly of my dear mother and father, and worry that they must think me dead. I remember how they were sleeping when I left the lodge house. I wanted to kiss Mother's cheek and whisper goodbye, but that would have woken her. Father slept with his arm about her, coughing slightly, but she was so used to it, she barely stirred. Dear Mother, what wouldn't I give to see your face before me, your smiling eyes. What wouldn't I give to hear your soft voice instead of the loud raucous sounds of this enemy! I spend many nights weeping quietly, even while Akaiyan sleeps.

Today, as I sweep out the dirt floor, the young Spanish soldier comes near. He lounges next to the door, leaning against its portal. He says nothing, but watches me work. When I'm done, I turn to clean the muddy boots and suddenly feel his hand upon my shoulder. I begin to tremble.

"What do you want?" I whisper in Croatoan, imagining the horror to come.

"*Inglés... inglés. Enséñame.*"

He points to his mouth, "*inglés*," and waves his hand.

"I can't teach you. No one must know."

"*Secreto.*"

"*¿Secreto? ¿Por qué?*"

He shrugs his shoulders. Who knows why this young

soldier wants to learn his enemy's language? Maybe for the same reason that I'm eager to learn fragments of Spanish, the way I can now speak fluent Croatoan.

I put my finger to my lips and he nods his head.

"*Un secreto.*"

"*Mi nombre es Enrique de Gomara.*"

"My name is Jess," I whisper back.

Chapter 20

Message From Spain

SEVERAL DAYS PASS and the young soldier learns his lessons well. He comes at night, this Enrique de Gomara, when all others are asleep. He creeps to the back of the hut where we're imprisoned and I whisper to him through the barred opening in the wall. Our hut is close to the woods and no one can see.

The risk is great for both of us. If caught, he'd surely be executed. As for me... I shudder to think of the consequences. Akaiyan warns me of the danger, but I'm compelled to continue. If I refuse, if I anger him, perhaps he'll tell them my secret. An English and a woman! I must make a friend amidst this enemy.

He's lonely, he tells me, longing for the sunny shores of a distant Spain. He was forced into service by a strict uncle. He misses his mother and his sisters, as I miss my mother and father, Thomas, Eleanor and little Virginia. He doesn't wish for anything more than companionship, a sweet smile, he says.

I want to believe him.

The garrison teems with activity. The Spanish ship is almost ready to sail. Cargo is loaded, timber cut, much the way we'd prepared John White's ship for its voyage back to England. I catch a sob in my throat whenever I think upon it, for John White has been delayed in his return for well over a year. Scattered fragments of news drift through the encampment, mainly that Philip's Armada is well placed in the English channel, poised to strike at England's heart.

All this means little to Akaiyan, who labors harder than I under the brutality of Pedro de Avilés. Nothing he does seems to please his Spanish taskmaster. Whippings are frequent and often, at night, I try to ease his pain by sponging him with water that Enrique manages to bring.

We're all prisoners, I truly believe, Akaiyan, myself and Enrique. He tells me in his poor English that he wants to flee this garrison and seek a way back to *España*, his home. I weep with him, for I long to break free from this hateful place and return to the beauty and serenity of my home on Croatoan Island.

It becomes harder and harder for Enrique to meet me at night. The *capitán* places more guards, for news has come of Indian war parties skulking through the region. Enrique has guard duty many nights. Then comes the most startling news of all.

"Philip has broken the *inglés'* back. Their ships are scattered. The proud queen kneels in homage to our king."

"Can this be true?" I ask Enrique when I get the chance.

"I do not know," he whispers back. "Another ship was seen at the mouth of the *Bahía de Santa Maria*. Our men rowed out to meet them. Perhaps we'll learn the truth soon."

Vicente González swaggers about the garrison, drunk

most of the time. He's been overheard telling the soldiers that Philip is already in the palace at London, that Elizabeth has surrendered.

I'm filled with a most terrible fear. For if Spain has, indeed, won against England, then what becomes of all our good ships, our supplies long overdue, our reinforcements held dockside until we're victorious? If this is true, what will become of us, Akaiyan and me, our brave colonists back on Croatoan Island, and the others who sailed for the Chesapeake over a year ago, though there's not been a sign of them? Will England join with Spain against France? Will Catholic Philip force Elizabeth into marriage, as was his bold intention from the beginning? Will England turn back to papal authority? So many questions and no answers!

"The Spanish come to rape and plunder this New World," I tell Enrique. "The English come to settle and build homes. That's the difference."

His eyes grow sad.

"The *conquistadores* say they serve God and His Majesty, give light to those who are in darkness, and grow rich, as all men desire to do. But this does not excuse the rape, the torture, the taking of lives."

He whispers urgently,

"I must return to *España*, see my mother and sisters once more. González sails shortly, to plunder the seas again. I don't wish to go."

"What can you do?"

"Escape."

And so we talk of it in whispered voices, in English, in Spanish and later, in Croatoan with Akaiyan.

"How can we escape?" he asks as I minister again to his bleeding back.

"I don't know. Enrique is desperate not to sail with González."

"I do not trust him."

"Why not?"

"He is not *caunotka,* he is not *nickreruroh.*"

"But he's like us in many ways. He's young...."

Akaiyan puts a finger to my lips.

"We will wait and see, *jureha.* There are many *squarrena* who wag their tails like *cheeth,* dogs. We will wait."

Chapter 21

Plans To Sail

"You're feeling good today."

The brown mare nuzzles my hand. I've found a special treat for her, some sugar left by my master on the table. I filled my pocket with some and have offered it while I'm brushing her. Her pink tongue licks my hand over and over.

"Enough. *Jureha,* I'll give you some more."

She whinnies low in her throat. She's due to foal in several weeks, and her belly is well-rounded. I never thought I could be drawn so to an animal. I love her deep brown eyes, her rich smell. I lean against her neck, my arms in an embrace.

"*Indio,*" and I hear the deep coarse voice of Vicente González. I turn with a gasp to see him standing by the post.

"You... like *los caballos?*"

"*Si,*" nodding my head. It pleases the Spanish to think I'm learning their language.

"I will take her with me on the ship. I pay de Avilés

mucha plata. I will have her and the foal."

In an instant he turns and is gone, leaving me to stand in shock. So he plans to take her with him, tied deep in the belly of his ship while he plunders the seas, gets caught in storms, until she weakens or miscarries her foal.

"I have a plan," I tell Akaiyan later that night. All day I've been thinking and thinking about it.

"What is it?"

"We will escape and take the brown *a hots* with us. I'll ride her far away. We'll take one for you, also."

He shakes his head.

"No, no, I can not ride."

"Yes, you can. It's not hard. I've seen them do it. Enrique will help us."

But Akaiyan just shakes his head. When I next see Enrique, I tell him of my plan. At first, he shakes his head, "No," like Akaiyan. But then as he thinks more on it, his eyes begin to gleam and he agrees.

"I will come with you. I'm a good rider. My father had *caballos en España.* I'll escape with you."

I'm filled now with this wild dream, to ride the *a hots* out of that garrison and head south once more, south toward Croatoan and my home. It consumes my very soul until I can hardly breathe. Is it possible? Can we trust Enrique? Dare we place our lives in the hands of a Spaniard, England's bitter enemy?

The news comes fast. Vicente González plans to set sail in two days. The ship is stocked with provisions, the holds have been readied for the brown mare and another black stallion. González pays de Avilés an exorbitant sum for both. And the worst news of all, he plans to take Akaiyan and me with him back to Spain, to be paraded as trophies at Philip's court. De Avilés grumbles and makes much protest, to have to give up his new-found slaves. But González knows his weakness; the gold coins and gems are dangled in front of *el capitán's* eyes. Reluctantly, he agrees.

"We must act tonight," I tell Enrique. "We can't wait another day. Tomorrow they will load, first the horses, then Akaiyan and myself."

Enrique hesitates.

"I don't know," he says. "I have guard duty. It will be difficult...."

"But you must," I implore. "It's our last chance."

That night, when we're locked into that hut, the chain around our ankles, I'm trembling with anxiety. What if Enrique can't get away to free us? What if he's been toying with me and even now, González and de Avilés know who I really am? What a prize I'll be for his soldiers on the high seas, to be stripped of my clothing in full view for all to see, to be violated over and over again....

We sit together in that rude hut, Akaiyan and I, holding each other, both afraid, both wondering if this will be our last night. He tells me he's not afraid to die, as long as it can be in battle. I tell him we won't die, that I trust Enrique. Even as I say it, fear rises like a stone in my throat.

The moon is hidden by thick clouds which will be in our favor, I think. I've hidden a small package of food in the stall near the brown mare. While alone with her these past several days, I've slipped the metal bit into her mouth and practiced sitting upon her back. I've made Akaiyan do the same with the black stallion. At first, he couldn't bring himself to mount. But with my urging, he finally got the courage. I'm sure he's the very first Croatoan to sit astride a horse. The black snorted and trembled at his scent, but then quieted down. Enrique will take another brown mare. Together we will lead them from the garrison under cover of darkness, then mount within the safety of the trees. González will be livid with anger. But with the ship due to sail, I'm hoping he won't take the time to track us down.

Chapter 22

The Raid

WE MANAGE TO DRIFT OFF into a restless sleep, but something awakens me. I've been dreaming of a young man, dressed in a strange costume. He appears before me, then begins a slow dance, much like the *unqua*. I can't see his face, but I'm not afraid in his presence. He reaches out to me, placing a hand upon my bodice. I awake with a start.

"Where is Enrique?" Akaiyan whispers. "The night passes."

He looks at me, sadness veiling his eyes, for he's been a disbeliever all along.

"He'll come," I tell him then, "he'll come, you'll see."

But I think perhaps Akaiyan may have been right, after all, for we've not heard a sound in several hours.

Then all of a sudden, a musket is fired, and another. Cries rend the air, more shots are heard, then the guttural sounds of Indian voices I don't recognize.

"Wa-hun-sen-a-cawh's braves!"

"Who?"

"The one the English call Powhatan. Wa-hun-sen-a-cawh. His warriors are raiding this garrison."

All around us, we can hear the cries of Spanish and Indian intermingled. Powhatan's hostiles have dared to attack. Our plans are in ruins.

I can smell smoke. The Indians are burning the Spanish huts. What about us? Will we be burned alive in this hut, chained at the ankles, unable to escape? I clutch Akaiyan. Just then, the door opens and a figure slips in. Is it an Indian? Or an angry Spaniard who's come to slit our throats in vengeance?

In the orange glow from the fires, I can see the glistening Savage standing before us. His face is painted with stripes of ochre and black. Feathers adorn his hair, giving him the look of an angry bird of prey. He carries a large *oosocke nauh*, knife. He grunts in surprise when he sees us, then raises his arm to strike. Before he can swing his arm, he grunts again and pitches forward, dead before he hits the ground. Behind him stands Enrique, his own *oosocke nauh* stained with blood.

"*Silencio*, I have the key," he whispers and I sigh with relief. I watch as he unlocks our chains.

"Come quickly. Now's our chance. We will get *los caballos* and ride out quickly."

Even in the dim light, I can see that he's wounded. But he grabs my hand as I grab Akaiyan's, and the three of us slip into the shadows at the back. The air is filled with cries and musket shots. The sky is orange with flames.

"Hurry, hurry," Enrique whispers. He pulls us toward the woods.

"The horses," I cry, "what about the horses?"

"They are waiting for us," he says. "I took them early

and tethered them. Come, come."

We step over fallen bodies, Indian and Spaniard. A hand grabs at my ankle and I almost scream.

"*Indio,*" a faint voice calls. "*Ayúdame.*"

I glance down to see Pedro de Avilés, a feathered arrow protruding from his chest. His eyes are glazing over.

"No," urges Enrique, "don't help him. Come, come, over here."

I shake my leg loose and leave the *capitán* as death steals across his face. The smoke from the fires covers our final run to the woodland. We reach the horses, who have been blindfolded. When I ask Enrique why, he replies,

"*Los caballos* are...afraid of fire. They would bolt unless I tied their eyes."

I bury my face in the brown mare's neck. She nuzzles my hand. The black stallion is nervous. His hide is lathered with sweat already. Enrique boosts me up upon the mare's back, my legs spread wide over her rounded sides. Akaiyan hesitates for but a moment, then jumps upon the stallion's back. Enrique mounts the other brown mare.

"Uncover their eyes and follow me," he whispers, and we do. He leads us deeper into the woods, away, far away from the smoke and the flames, the screams and the shots. The *a hots* move nervously, the stallion side-stepping. I can see that Akaiyan is having a difficult time with him.

"Enrique," I call as loudly as I dare, "change horses with Akaiyan."

It's easy to see that Enrique is an expert horseman, for once upon the black, he's in complete control. I hope that Akaiyan's pride is not too injured by the change, but I don't have time to reflect. We guide the *a hots* through thick trees and over fallen branches. None of us can move fast. The orange sky above the Spanish garrison fades into the background. Thick black clouds cover the moon, a good omen. We move as quickly as Enrique dares, and not a word is spoken.

We travel this way for two hours, moving at a quick trot. The woods are too thick for us to gallop. I can see that Akaiyan is being sorely bounced around, for he is no horseman. I pull the brown mare so that she drops back to keep pace with him.

"Press your legs firmly against her sides. Rise up and down as she moves."

He glances at me, a pained expression on his face. When he sees that I'm doing the same thing as Enrique, he quickly understands and copies our movements. After that, the rest of our journey is more comfortable for him.

Chapter 23

Escape

WE TRAVEL ON AND ON, ever southward, through thick trees and brush which makes the going difficult for the *a hots*. Thorns reach out to scratch their sides and tear at our hair. The black stallion and the two mares are lathered with exhaustion before Enrique decides to stop.

"We will rest...*un rato,*" he says, combining both English and Spanish in his own peculiar way. "Then we must move again."

He points to the sky. Already the night is paling before the advance of dawn. We must be well away from the Spanish garrison and Powhatan's braves before *heita* rises in the east.

I'm glad to stop, for riding chafes the inside skin of my thighs and legs. Enrique leads the horses down to a tiny stream where he lets them drink. Then he tethers them and we all rest. After about fifteen minutes, it's Akaiyan who urges us to move again.

"Keep going," he says to me. "We must leave no *wauh-*

hauhne, path, for them to follow."

"Haven't we gone far enough?"

He shakes his head.

"We must not stop. If they find us, they will kill us all."

And so we mount up and ride again, this time at a gallop, for the trees have thinned somewhat. We ride with *hoonoch,* the wind, at our heels, pushing us onward, deeper south, deeper into the unknown.

I know we're going south, but that's all. We zig-zag through the clearings and open spaces, never staying in a straight line. Sometimes we head away from the sea, deep inland, then Enrique suddenly veers east.

When the sun is half-way climbing to its meridian, we find a large outcrop of rock and tether the horses inside. Then we fling ourselves down and sleep overtakes us. My legs ache and I catch Akaiyan rubbing his, also. Enrique smiles.

"After a while, your legs will not hurt so much," he says.

"It's not just my legs," I say to Akaiyan in Croatoan, feeling sore all over.

"We will stay here until dark," Akaiyan motions to Enrique, who nods in agreement. "We will move at night."

"Why *oosottoo?*"

"Because the soldiers are *wattattoo watse,* lazy fellows. At night, they will sleep. We will run!"

We ride throughout the night again, listening to the howls of the *squarrena.* This makes the *a hots* nervous and fretful, and we all have difficulty keeping them in rein. But we spur them onward. I imagine González's men riding through the woodlands hard upon our trail, the pounding of their horses' hooves matching the pounding, pounding of my heart.

"*Mucha plata* for the *soldado* who captures *los indios,*" González cries. "*¡Entonces los mataremos!*"

91

Akaiyan leans his body into the wind, pressing his knees against his mare's heaving flanks. He's learned much from watching Enrique, riding better now, moving as one with his horse.

By dawn of the second day, we rest again, eating some of the dried strips of meat I packed away, then drinking from a small *awoo*. I think of the stream that ran behind our timbered houses back on Roanoak; I think of Agnes, of George Howe, of his father so cruelly murdered. I think of my dear mother and father, Eleanor and little Virginia. I remember Ananyas and how calm and wise he always was. A lump chokes my throat and tears run down my cheeks.

"Oh, Little Bird," Akaiyan brushes them away. "Do not cry. Soon we will be home."

And what is home to all of us? To me, it's the Indian village I've grown to love, the women stirring the cooking pots while they sing, the babes toddling about the camp, belonging to all the village. It's the children taking lessons from Eleanor, the hunters bringing home a deer they've tracked, the wind blowing from the sea with its fresh salt smell.

To Enrique, home must be a sunny land far across the western ocean, a land he remembers as a child, no wars, no savagery. He's told me of the gleaming whitewashed buildings, the fields where the farmers sow their crops. Surely the *España* of his youth is much like the England I remember?

I've tended his wounded shoulder, where an arrow pierced the flesh. Akaiyan pulled the shaft out, while Enrique bit down hard on a piece of leather. Then I cleansed the wound with water, placed *auoona hau*, moss, over it and bandaged it. After two days, the flesh is healing and there's no infection.

We ride again through the night, a full moon painting the woodlands in silver. Akaiyan, who's been leading the way, pulls up his horse at one point and signals us to dismount. We crouch low in the brush, holding the *a hots'* muzzles as a raiding party of Weapemeoc skulks through the woods to our far right, off in the distance, scouting for whatever trophies they seek. I'm glad then that Akaiyan knows these woods so well, for Enrique or I would have ridden right into their midst. The animals are glad for the rest, and make no sound. The brown mare lowers her head to graze.

Chapter 24

The Chesapeake Colony

"WHAT ARE THESE RUINS?"

"A settlement," says Akaiyan. "*Nickreruroh.* See, here is *au-nuka,* axe and over here...."

"An *ocnock.*"

"What's that?" asks Enrique, peering over my shoulder.

"A cooking pot," I answer, my eyes beginning to fill with tears. For surely we've discovered the remains of an English encampment, badly overgrown with vegetation. Remnants of community are scattered about: a kettle, several shirts torn and fouled with the elements, a *trossa,* hat, some bowls, a bent spoon, even an *ootic caugh-ne,* mortar and *tic-caugh-ne,* pestle. Burned shells of houses remain standing, but they're empty and devoid of life. There once were families here, cooking, living in homes, their *woccanookne,* children, playing....

I sink to my knees, my head in my hands.

"*Ut-tewots?*" Akaiyan asks. "How many families?"

"I don't know," shaking my head. "Many. This was home to many of my people."

He kneels down next to me, holding me tightly. I can't help but sob bitterly in his arms. Enrique paces back and forth, not knowing what to do.

For we've stumbled upon what was once a small colony of English men and women, and I don't know who they were. There are no bodies to identify, nothing. My spirit is wracked with pain. We've traveled five days now on the backs of our swift horses. The Spanish garrison was located high up the Baye on the western side. We've ridden down its length, crossed several large *awoo* where the horses were almost swept off their feet and still, we haven't left the Chesapeake lands. Many times, we've had to backtrack and turn inland to avoid finger-like projections of sea sweeping in across the grass and sand. This is a land of water: inlets, rivers, gushing streams, small bays, all have hindered our passage south.

And now this colony lies in ruin before us, an oasis fallen to the wilderness, once home to men and women and children. An axe rests still in the uncut limb of a tree. I close my eyes and visualize George Howe, perhaps, cutting timber with Roger Prat and the others, building a new home as was his father's dream. Could this be where they settled? Somehow, it seems smaller than the colony we'd created on Roanoak. Fifty-four people had sailed on the pinnace to try and form the Cittie of Ralegh as originally planned. This settlement was not built for that many people; perhaps twenty-five in all had lived here. Why would they have split into two groups? That would have been foolhardy. And where are the remaining colonists? Oh, my head is spinning!

We spend a day and night in this unhappy place. Akai-yan and Enrique want to travel on, but I can't, not yet. I must seek answers and try to learn what happened. I walk the overgrown tangle of weeds, exploring as best I can each burned-out shell of lodging. Perhaps I'll find some clue as to who once lived here.

There are no bodies, no graves as far as I can determine. It's as if they all disappeared suddenly, without a trace. Yet, there was violence done, for the fire-damaged homes attest to it. I find piles of stacked wood in several places outside, wood for the cold winter which is now upon us. A child's bed stands in one home, the bedding pulled up neatly as if just made. The ashes of their cooking fires are long cold but if I close my eyes, I can see the women calling the men and children to supper, hear the sounds of quiet prayer asking God's blessing before they eat, the echo of children's laughter.

Where is George Howe, Ambrose Viccar the younger, John and the other boys? Where is Roger Prat and Dionys and Margaret Harvye with their babe, Christopher? Suddenly, without caring, I begin to run blindly through the woods, crying out, tripping over roots and whipped by thorns. I will run until my heart stops beating in my breast, if Akaiyan doesn't catch up with me, pulling me savagely into his arms, forcing me down upon my knees, wracked with grief.

He whispers to me in words of the *unqua*, holding me against his beating heart.

"Little Bird, Little Bird, weep *kahunk*, now. Tomorrow we will travel on. There is only pain here. *Untah hah?*"

I nod my head, leaning my face upon his shoulder until the beating of my heart lessens, until my body no longer convulses with tears, for he is the source of my strength. I feel his calmness flowing into me, his love diffusing into my blood, my bones. He raises my face and softly kisses my lips.

"*Merrauka*," he whispers, "we will forget this place.

There is a home that awaits you far to the south, the home of my people, your people, full of love and peace."

Chapter 25

Mother's Brooch

TRY AS HE MIGHT, Akaiyan can't get me to leave this place of ruins. I have no will to move on. Perhaps because memories of the Spanish garrison are still so fresh in my mind, this sad place has taken on a special meaning. Where once I was eager to leave the English settlement on Roanoak, now I cling to this lonely, God-forsaken spot. Everywhere I turn, I'm reminded of an English past; even the torn remnant of my beloved flag fluttering uselessly from its post is a call for tears to spring forth anew.

"Lyon of England," I weep softly, "you fly no more in the breeze. Oh, what's happened to your brave adventurers? What's happened to their dreams, their passions? Where are they now, your cubs who are scattered to the winds?"

During these sad moments, Akaiyan can't console me. He watches for signs of an enemy, Spanish or Weapemeoc, ever alert to danger. Enrique keeps guard with him. They pace the perimeters, eyes searching the deep woods for movement, ears tuned for the snap of a twig, the crack of a dried leaf. They can't communicate, for neither knows the other's tongue, but they're as one in their bond to protect me.

Nor do they understand the depth of my grief. I weep for Ananyas, buried in a forgotten, shallow grave. I weep for Eleanor and her empty heart. I weep for sweet Agnes, for John Tydway, for all whose dreams died too soon.

When the sun has risen on the third day, Akaiyan comes to me with hands outstretched.

"We must leave *kahunk,* now."

"*Connauwox,* I'm sick."

"It is in your mind."

"And my heart."

"You will not heal until you leave this place. You will be a *cusquerre,* old woman, unless we ride away."

"One last walk," I entreat, "to say goodbye."

But to whom am I saying goodbye? I don't even know who these people were. I wander one last time through the desolate ruins, until I come to the last house. It's on the fringe of woodland, furthest from the central community. Whose house was it? Maybe a father, mother and two children.... But stop, I caution myself, these thoughts can only bring more tears.

The roof is half-burned away, the walls barely standing. Two beds, blackened from flames, are up-ended against the one remaining wall, as if someone hurled them in anger. I scuff the dirt floor, filled with fallen leaves and debris. This settlement has been in ruins for several months. So when did this attack take place, September, October? Did the people flee to safety and, even now, are building homes further south? Or did they all die in that one savage attack? If so, where are the bodies? Where are the graves?

99

My foot hits something half-covered by dirt, and I bend to pick it up. My hand flies to my mouth. For it's Mother's brooch, given by her to Margaret Harvye the day she left with the others for the Chesapeake. I remember how Mother pinned it gently upon her shawl, saying it would bring her luck. Mistress Harvye wept as she left, looking over her shoulder to the woods' edge where Agnes was buried. She clutched the babe Christopher to her breast as if she'd never let him go.

The brooch is scratched and the filigree around its edges caked with dirt. Strange, but I have no more tears left as I gently rub the cameo surface and clean the earth away. When I'm finished, it shines almost the way it did when Mother wore it. I carefully pin it upon my buckskin bodice and turn to go.

"We must leave," Akaiyan says, leading me back to where Enrique holds the horses. He helps me mount the brown mare, then jumps skillfully upon his *a hots'* back. Enrique mounts the black stallion, reining him tightly, and we're off.

"What is that you are wearing?" Akaiyan asks, pulling up his mare next to mine.

"Mother's brooch," I reply. "She gave it to Mistress Harvye before they left for the Chesapeake."

"There are no dead people," he shakes his head, "there are no graves."

"Maybe they're still alive."

I tap my mare's sides. She bucks a little, then settles down to a slow canter. We head south again, leaving questions unanswered, thoughts unspoken.

Chapter 26

Enrique

ENRIQUE SITS TALL in the saddle, holding the reins of the black stallion lightly in his hands. Our horses were saddled when we first left the garrison, but now only Enrique and I ride the thick Spanish *montura*. After one hour, Akaiyan unbuckled the cinch and threw it off, preferring to ride bareback. He's become quite adept at guiding the mare using the pressure of his knees, the subtle movement of his body. Enrique comments that he seems born to ride *los caballos*, which I've told Akaiyan is a true compliment, coming from a Spaniard.

The English settlement has been left far behind, its pain already fading. I'm now convinced that its inhabitants are, indeed, safe in some other place, re-building their homes, their lives. I wish it to be true; I pray it is, for that thought sustains me. I couldn't bear the idea of harm befalling Margaret and Dyonis Harvye and their babe, Christopher, nor any of the others. I don't even know if George Howe was with them.

Perhaps they knew of an impending attack and had already fled to safety under cover of night, leaving one brave colonist behind to torch their homes. The hostiles, or the Spanish, would have been met with the same desolation that greeted us. Each would have assumed the other was responsible.

We're nearing that part of the coast which will lead directly to the outer strip of land buffeting the sea. Our journey will end soon, Akaiyan says, for the *a hots* have wings on their hooves. I notice the brown mare is becoming more and more uncomfortable, and I just hope we can arrive at our destination before her pangs of labor begin. We stop to rest more frequently, for she breathes heavily. For the last hour, I have ridden behind Akaiyan on his mare, clutching his waist. We've tied an *utsera* between both mares. Enrique said she needed less weight as she's carrying enough with her foal. Even so, she seems dispirited, and we feel her time is near.

We've seen no sign of Weapemeoc or Spanish. Enrique believes that even if González had come after us, we had a good head start. He wouldn't have lost his silver payment either, for de Avilés was dead. By now, Vicente González should be sailing the high seas, searching for English ships. Enrique has said many thankful prayers in Spanish for his deliverance from that evil man, and I've joined him. At those times Akaiyan leaves us alone, respecting our need to meditate.

After prayers while Akaiyan stands watch, Enrique has begun to tell me of his family. His father died when he was a babe. His mother came under the protective custody of his *tío*, a mean-spirited man.

"You remind me... *a mis hermanas,*" he says, and I'm rather glad I'm like his sisters. All of them knew a desolate childhood, with many lessons and little time for play. His only enjoyment was riding *los caballos,* for his uncle insisted upon his learning equestrian skills. Enrique has a natural ability with horses, *"una gran pasión,"* he says. I can see it in the way he handles the stallion, who is always fretful and difficult. The mare Akaiyan rides is a gentle animal, able and willing. But it's with my sweet brown *a hots* that his love shines through. Whenever we rest, he's always caressing her, stroking her soft, velvet nose, whispering in her ear, feeding her a little grain, finding whatever scraps of grass are still on the ground.

"Mi querida y bella yegua," he says, "my dear and beautiful mare."

One time, he held my hand palm-down upon her rounded belly, much the way I'd once felt Eleanor's babe in her womb. She nickered softly and let me. I could feel the movement of the unborn foal, the kick of a tiny hoof against my hand. Surely God's wonder is everywhere, even with the animals! Enrique says the foal comes from the black stallion. It's at this time that Akaiyan joins us admiring the *a hots,* awed beyond belief at their power and majesty.

"Never have I moved so fast," he tells me. "We fly like the wind."

"Hoonoch" is faster," I laugh. He smiles and my heart skips a beat. It's been a long time since I've seen him smile. He leans down to kiss me, a familiar and most welcome thing. Enrique is watching us and I wonder if he's ever loved a girl.

"Yo estuve enamorado una vez," he says later, "but she is betrothed now to another."

"Wouldn't she wait for you?"

"No, her parents... *no lo permitirían.* I went off to sea and she...." His voice trails off.

I stare at this young Spanish *soldado,* alone in an alien

land like me. The difference between us is that I was eager to set sail from England, surrounded by the love of my family, while he was forced into servitude by his uncle. He stands before me in his Spanish uniform, a symbol of England's bitterest adversary; I face him as Spain's *peor enemigo,* worst enemy. He's almost twenty, the same age as Akaiyan who is, supposedly, the enemy of us both. Yet... we're becoming friends.... Our different backgrounds and cultures mean nothing here in this wilderness, for we need each other. Joined together on a pilgrimage to the southland, we seek safety, the fulfillment of our dreams, and what we hope is peace once more.

Chapter 27

The Foaling

TOWARD EVENING, we ride into a clearing. It's been a long day and my brown mare is tired. Her head droops wearily, even though I haven't been riding her for an entire day. Enrique tethers the *a hots*, feeding them some of the grain he's managed to save from what he brought with him. There's precious little left. We dismount and sink gratefully to the ground. Then Akaiyan points.

"Look," he whispers. "This is the place of the *whaharia,* dead. The graves are here."

I strain to see where he's looking. In the dimming light, I can see two small crosses planted in the ground. Immediately, I jump up to run over.

"Wait," Akaiyan cautions. "*Oonutsauka,* remember what happened."

So I wait impatiently, while he and Enrique scout the area. They're gone a long time. When they finally return, Akaiyan nods his head.

"There are no Spanish here. *Its warke,* you may go safely."

But I don't run, after all. Instead, I approach with a strange trepidation. I haven't got Eleanor's Bible to read the passages from, nor do I have her silver wedding band. I stop half-way to the first cross.

"What is wrong?" Akaiyan asks.

"I don't have the Bible to say prayers over his grave."

Akaiyan glances at Enrique, who shrugs at first, then comes slowly forward.

"This is for you," he says, and hands me a torn and rain-soaked book of God's prayer.

"But where did you get this?"

"I found it back at *el campamento de los ingleses.* It was in one of the houses, so I picked it up."

I take the Bible from him.

"And this is also for you," and he brings forth from his shirt pocket Eleanor's ring which I'd given him. He holds it up in the fading light.

"*Un anillo bonito,*" he says sadly, "but not mine to keep."

He thrusts it at me and strides back to the horses. I approach the cross. Sure enough, carved roughly on its surface are the words, 'Ananyas Dare, 1588.' A sob rises in my throat, threatening to choke me.

"Oh, Ananyas," I whisper, kneeling down and beginning to weep. I take the Bible and turn to some passages. The ink has smeared throughout the pages and it's hard to read. I try to remember what special verses Eleanor had marked and when I can't, say the "Our Father" and the "Twenty-Third Psalm."

"The Lord is my shepherd, I shall not want...." When

I'm finished I get up, turning once more to Akaiyan and Enrique.

"Can we bring him back?"

At first, they don't understand what I'm asking. I search for the words in both Croatoan and Spanish, but they're shaking their heads. Finally, I run back to the grave and pantomime digging up the body. Enrique says "no!" most emphatically. Akaiyan just stares, for he's known all along that my purpose was to try and bring Ananyas home.

A loud moaning sound draws our attention. The brown mare has sunk to the ground, her eyes wide with terror. Already, a sweat lathers her body. She's in labor.

Enrique moves the other *a hots* away and comes running back to the mare. He cradles her head in his arms.

"*Bella yegua, bella yegua,*" he whispers.

I'm drawn with fascination to this most natural scene, remembering vividly when Eleanor gave birth to Virginia. Akaiyan kneels down to assist Enrique. He strokes her heaving sides. The mare groans again.

"*Es su primero,* her first," Enrique says, a tone of concern in his voice. "We must help her."

The birth of a foal is surely the most wondrous thing to behold. Where I remember the human birth to be frightening and somewhat long, this foal comes swiftly into our world. The mare relaxes under Enrique's gentle touch. Within a few minutes, the forelegs and head appear, covered in a membrane. Enrique quickly clears its tiny nostrils. The body follows, slipping out easily. The tiny thing flops its head and stares at me, unseeing, yet looking deep into my soul. I am one with God's tiny creature lying before me. The mare immediately turns her head toward her child and struggles to get up. She lowers her head and begins licking the foal with

109

her pink tongue.

"It's a filly," laughs Enrique, "*una hembra,* like you."

I hug him, then Akaiyan, who hasn't stopped staring at this miracle of life. He raises his outspread arms to the sky.

"Oh, Great Spirit," he calls, "we give thanks to you for this *a hots* which lives and breathes."

The foal tries to stand on its unsteady legs. With help from Enrique and Akaiyan, it finally wobbles to its feet, seeks out the mare's milk and begins suckling. The night has fallen silently, yet we hear music all around us: the hoot of an owl, the howl of a distant *squarrena.* Stars sparkle in the winter sky. The mare snorts softly under Enrique's touch, turning her head to lick the rump of her baby. Akaiyan holds my hand.

"Over there is death; here is life."

"I prefer life," I whisper, stroking the little *a hots'* warm body, glancing over my shoulder at the two wooden crosses.

Chapter 28

Ananyas's Grave

NONE OF US CAN TAKE OUR eyes off the baby foal. After her first few hesitant steps, she walks more steadily and suckles eagerly at the mare's milk. Her tiny tail whisks back and forth.

"She is a beauty," Enrique marvels. "See the star on her forehead."

Akaiyan hasn't stopped staring at her. For an *unqua* who's never seen horses before this journey, the birth of this tiny *a hots* must seem a miracle.

"What shall we call her?" I ask Enrique.

"I don't know," he replies. "Let Akaiyan name her. *Ella puede pertenecerle*, she belongs to him."

When I translate Enrique's Spanish words into Croatoan, Akaiyan's face lights up.

"You give her to me? I have never owned such a creature. Imagine what my father will say! Imagine what they will all say!"

He thinks for a moment, looking first at her, then at the heavens.

"I shall call her *uttewiraratse*, for the stars in the sky."

"What a long name," I laugh.

"What would you call her?"

"Let's just call her Star, for that's what her name means."

Akaiyan nods his head.

"A good name."

Star suckles while the brown mare licks her over and over. When she's had enough, she folds her legs under and settles in a small, contented heap. Soon she's asleep. Enrique keeps watch while Akaiyan and I close our eyes. Before we know it, Enrique is shaking us awake.

"It is almost first light," he whispers. "We must find a safer place to rest."

"What about Ananyas's body?" is the first thing I ask.

Akaiyan shakes his head.

"It is bad luck to disturb the graves of those who have died. It will bring evil down upon us."

"I think it is a bad idea, also," adds Enrique. "The dead should rest in peace. And the ground is too hard to dig up. If his body wasn't properly prepared for burial, then it will be in bad condition. This will cause problems if *los lobos* come close."

I stare at them, torn between Akaiyan's belief, the truth of what Enrique says, and the emotions of my heart. How shall I tell Eleanor? They stand there watching me.

"Then I'll say more prayers over his body," I answer finally, "and dig a hole to place Eleanor's ring."

They wait as I read several of my own favorite passages above Ananyas's grave, and over Master Spendlove's as well. Then with Enrique's *oosocke nauh*, I dig a hole as deep as I can in the cold ground and place Eleanor's silver wedding band in it. I gently cover the ring with earth and pat it down.

"I hope this is above your heart, dear Ananyas," I whisper. "For you and sweet Eleanor are bound for all eternity."

Tears are rolling down my cheeks as we mount upon the *a hots*. The brown mare is once again tied to our mare, and the foal trots loosely after her.

"Do not cry, Little Bird," says Akaiyan, feeling my arms about his waist, "for you have done all you could for your friend. I am sure his spirit is now with the gods, for he was a good and just man. If he were *unqua*, he might have been a great chief."

I take one last look at the two wooden crosses jutting forlornly above the half-frozen earth. Two brave men lie there, I think to myself, two hearts which once beat in warm bodies, two hearts which loved others and were loved in return. Such sadness fills me that I lay my head against Akaiyan's shoulder, closing my eyes until we have left that place of sorrows. I only hope that Eleanor will understand why we couldn't bring him home.

We move slowly, for the tiny *a hots* can't go very fast. After less than an hour, Akaiyan pulls up the reins and jumps off, checking to see that little Star is all right. He's most solicitous, petting and stroking her, admiring her perfection. She has four white stockinged feet, a broomstick of a tail, and that perfect star set above her eyes. She's a deep brown color. Enrique has told us she'll probably be a bay when she's grown, trying to explain in Spanish and broken English the rich mahogany hue. The black stallion has sniffed casually at her, until the brown mare laid back her ears and nipped him sharply on the rump. How we laughed.

"He makes the baby and then she will not let him near," chuckles Enrique.

We are lucky to find a thick grove of trees near a small stream. We tether the *a hots*, watching in delight as Star suckles once more. Already, she moves steadily on her long legs, for the mare's milk is rich and satisfying.

We stay at rest for the remainder of the day, sheltered by the trees, watching the foal and delighting in her. She has no fear of any of us, coming to our soft call, letting us rub behind her ears and stroke her neck. Akaiyan marvels that she will grow to such a size that she can carry a man on her back. The brown mare has quickly recovered from the birthing, and is most caring of her babe. She smells her constantly, alternately licking and nuzzling her. The other mare seems content just to watch the whole procedure. And the black stallion keeps his distance, in deference to the brown mare's teeth.

Chapter 29

Un Demonio Del Infierno

IN THE DREAM I'm riding Star, who is now a full-grown horse. We ride swiftly, covering miles and miles of open fields. I can feel the wind in my face, stinging my eyes. My body settles into the rhythm and flow of Star's gallop. We're as one, horse and rider, *a hots* and *unqua*. We could leave the dull earth and climb toward the brilliant heavens, for nothing is impossible.

"Oh, Star," I whisper in my dream. "How I love you."

She whinnies an answer. I lean down to pet her neck, throwing my arms around her, burying my face in her flowing mane. Then I hear a rough voice. It's neither Enrique nor Akaiyan. The dream fades even as I wish it to last forever. Rough hands seize me and pull me upward. I awaken to see four Savages gleaming in the moonlight, surrounding me and Akaiyan. He's held prisoner by the largest of them. Painted stripes adorn their faces.

"Weapemeoc!" I gasp.

"Be silent," Akaiyan cautions in Croatoan before one of them clouts the side of his head. We're alone in the clearing; Enrique and the horses are nowhere in sight.

The Savages speak in a dialect I can't understand. They gesture, and it's very clear that they're arguing about what to do with us. Their heads are shorn close at the sides, like the Savage who tried to attack us in the hut at the Spanish garrison. Lines of brown and crimson zig-zag down their cheeks. Their eyes are circled in black. Altogether, they're a fearsome sight.

I try to catch Akaiyan's eye, but it's impossible. The Savages keep us separated. One of them, a huge fellow, is taking out his knife. He spits upon the earth and waves the *oosocke nauh* in Akaiyan's face. I wonder how the *unqua* can be such fierce enemies, when they're created by the same Great Spirit. I want to cry out to Akaiyan, but rough hands seize me and push me against a tree.

The Savages turn their attention to Akaiyan. The one with the knife raises it high in the air, poised to strike. Akaiyan stands there bravely, his lip running blood, his eyes unwavering. At that very moment, a piercing cry fills the air. The Savages turn in its direction. From the silvered woods, a ghostly figure appears riding the big black stallion. It's Enrique!

He waves his knife in the air, giving loud whoops and war cries in Spanish. The stallion rears, pawing the air with his sharp hooves. With a thunderous bellow, Enrique rides the stallion right into our midst. The Savages drop their knives and scatter in all directions. They must think he's a monster from *popogusso!* Without a backward glance, they disappear into the woods, cries of fear echoing behind them. Enrique rides the stallion around in great circles, first north, then east, west and south. He makes the stallion rear high in the air, again and again. The stallion is white-lathered and his breath snorts out in clouds of steam.

It takes several minutes for Enrique to get the black under control. Finally he stands there trembling, while Enrique quickly dismounts and strokes his neck. Then he tethers him and comes toward us.

"They think I am a *monstruo*," he smiles. "Horse and man as one. *Un demonio del infierno*."

Akaiyan wipes his mouth and runs over to me.

"Are you well?" he asks.

"Just frightened. Where did they come from?"

"I was leading *los caballos* to water. I saw them tracking through the woods. I tied the horses and waited. When I saw what they were doing, I jumped upon the stallion." He laughs. *"¡Aquí estoy yo!"*

I throw my arms about his neck.

"You saved us. They were going to kill Akaiyan."

"They have never seen the *a hots* before. Not even a small one."

"And my fierce black Diablo is not small," Enrique smiles. "He would frighten any one."

"Oh, Diablo," I run to him and pet his soft nose. He snorts and lowers his head for me to scratch behind his ears.

"For you he is not *el diablo*. *Tú le gustas*, he likes you."

"Why didn't you wake us to go with you."

"Ah, you were sleeping so soundly, it would have been a pity to disturb you."

I shudder at the thought of the Savages and what they'd almost done to Akaiyan. What if Enrique hadn't seen them slipping through the night? What if they'd killed us both and waited for Enrique? Would they have killed the *a hots* also?

Would they have killed Star?

"Where are the horses?" I ask impatiently.

"*Están seguros...* safe," Enrique replies. "Hidden in the thicket near the stream."

"Let's go," and I start to run.

Akaiyan grabs my arm.

"Wait," he says. "They will not be back. They think we are evil."

"How do you know?"

"*Connaugh jost twane.* All of them were drunk. Could you not smell their breath?"

"They will have *pesadillas* for days," laughs Enrique.

"They will go back to their people and tell them about this place, that it is worse than a nightmare. They will be much *werricauna.*"

My heart is still beating fast. So much has happened, surely I can't stand another thing. Akaiyan comes over and puts his arm around me.

"Little Bird, what is wrong?"

"I want to go home," I whisper. "I want to go home... to our people."

Chapter 30

Crossing The Water

I KEEP THINKING OF poor Eleanor, and how sorry I am that we couldn't bring Ananyas's body back to Croatoan Island. However, the idea of digging up a dead body and transporting it across miles is not a pleasant one. In truth, when we left the island so many weeks ago, I hadn't thought about any of the consequences: Spaniards and hostiles attacking us, wolves stalking, or the terrible condition the corpse might be in. Akaiyan had tried to warn me, but I didn't listen. I'm still a child in so many ways. I wonder if I'll ever grow up!

The little *a hots* trots quickly beside her mother but even so, we rest often during the night hours, allowing her to suckle and regain her strength. Already she's growing, frolicking about and making us laugh. It's so good to be able to laugh again, especially after our harrowing experience with the Weapemeoc. Since Enrique gave Star to him, Akaiyan looks upon the young *soldado* with a new regard. He's even begun trying to learn some Spanish, but Akaiyan has no patience with language. He much prefers that I act as translator. I find that I'm becoming more fluent in Spanish and that delights me. Who'd have thought I'd be able to converse in anything other than English!

On our third night, we reach the large body of water separating the banks from the mainland. It seems to stretch for miles. Akaiyan tries to remember where he and Skotai had hidden the *ooshunnawa*, and it takes him several scouting excursions before he finally uncovers it.

"Over here," he calls excitedly.

I wonder whether the *ooshunnawa* will do us any good. What about the horses? They certainly wouldn't fit. If we didn't have Star, they could possibly swim behind us. What will we do with the little *hembra?*

Akaiyan and Enrique engage in much conversation, one in Spanish, the other in Croatoan. Somehow they manage to communicate, though I'm sure I don't know how for I'm busy with the foal, playing with her, stroking her. Enrique comes to me.

"We will use *soga* and tether *los caballos* behind the canoe. We'll build a harness for Star, then attach her to the brown mare. Then we'll *flotarla por el agua*."

Floating her seems an impossible idea, but Akaiyan and Enrique set quickly to work. Akaiyan takes the long *utsera* that Enrique brought with him, making shorter ropes from its length. Enrique cuts small branches from pine trees with his *oosocke nauh* and, using some *utsera* and the leather from his belt, makes a weird sort of contraption to hold Star's head above water. When he's finished, we practice by placing it over her head. She can't escape. At first, she snorts wildly and bucks away. Akaiyan soothes her and she calms under his touch. After a few tries, the foal accepts the head harness,

though the whites of her eyes flash continuously. It's hard not
to smile at this tiny creature wearing the strange thing of wood,
rope and leather.

"But won't the others drown?" I ask Akaiyan, imagining
the horses sinking below the waves.

Enrique answers.

"*Los caballos* can swim well. They have been known to
swim to shore from a sinking ship."

I stare out at the expanse of water, the sun sparkling upon
the surface. It's really not that far, I think to myself. Enrique
and Akaiyan will row hard and fast, while I watch the horses.
All Star will have to do is keep her head above the water.

We tie the ropes to the horses, the black stallion first so
he can help to pull the others. Then Akaiyan's mare and,
finally, my brown *a hots* and Star. Enrique practices leading
the black into the shallows time and again, until he gets used
to the water washing against his legs. Then he does the same
with the others. All of them take reasonably well to entering
the water. Except for Star! She kicks and plunges when she
feels the wetness on her body.

"*Esto no va a ser fácil,* this isn't easy," Enrique grunts,
trying to hold her still. The brown mare is most concerned for
her babe. She keeps whinnying and looking back. Finally,
Enrique signals us to get into the canoe. He pushes us off,
then pulls on the rope of the black and the mares. They enter
the water, moving out with us. Enrique picks up the foal in
his arms, wades out up to his waist and lowers her gently in
the water. She kicks a little, looking to Enrique for her
salvation. He stays with her until she gets accustomed to the
buoyancy and begins moving her legs.

"She seems all right," he calls to us, waiting a few
moments longer. Then he swims out to the canoe and climbs

on board.

"*Vamos*," he says, picking up an oar. We move slowly away from the shoreline, a strange entourage: *nickreruroh*, *unqua* and Spanish, with four *a hots* strung out in a line behind us. The black strikes out with his powerful legs, swimming strongly and pulling the others. The two mares feel his tremendous thrust and follow suit, kicking their legs and swimming. All the way behind the brown mare, the little bay *yegüita* is bobbing up and down in the waves, head resting on the branches of her harness, eyes wide with fright, but floating!

Chapter 31

Rescue

IN THE MIDDLE OF THE WATERS, the harness slips off
Star's head. I'm the first one to notice. I can see the branches
still floating on the surface, but no foal.

"Enrique!" I scream, "where's Star?"

He drops the paddle and scrambles over to me, searching
the sea.

"Over there," he points and I strain my eyes. Star has
drifted far away from the brown mare, her head barely above
the level of the water. It's clear that she's in trouble.

Enrique tears off his jacket and plunges into the sea. The
black stallion is still churning the water strongly, snorting in
great gulps of air. Enrique narrowly misses the powerful thrust
of his legs. He swims strongly in the direction of the little filly.
I can hear the brown mare now, calling to her baby. Akaiyan
rows more slowly, but keeps the *ooshunnawa* headed straight
for the far side, which I can now see in the distance.

It takes Enrique but a few moments to reach Star, just

before her head disappears beneath the swell. He grabs her tufted mane and pulls her up. Somehow he manages to swim toward us with one hand, while his other supports and lifts her. The little *a hots* is almost drowned and makes choking sounds.

"*¡Apúrate!*" Enrique gasps upon reaching us. "Help me lift her."

We can't do it without Akaiyan, who pulls with me while Enrique pushes her limp body into the bottom of the canoe. Water is streaming out of her mouth.

"She's dead!" I cry.

Enrique pulls himself into the canoe.

"Help her," he orders. "Turn her on her side. Push the *agua* out of her body."

But the little *a hots* isn't dead after all. I push lightly on her chest while more water trickles from her mouth. In a moment, her legs begin to kick and she raises her head. She struggles to get up, but Enrique covers her with his jacket and keeps her down.

"Don't let her stand," he says. "Keep her quiet. *¿Puedes hacer eso?*"

"Yes," and I put my arms about Star's neck. "Sweet little babe, little *a hots*, you almost didn't make it, did you?"

We row steadily after that, as fast as we can. I can see Enrique and Akaiyan are getting tired, and so are the three horses still in the water. The black still swims strongly, but the mares are weakening. More and more, I can see their heads sinking lower in the water.

"Hurry, hurry, they can't swim much longer."

I've rubbed the filly as dry as I can, and she is wide-eyed with fear. But she listens to my voice and lies still under my touch. I have covered her with kisses from her nose to her rump.

Even the black stallion is weakening as our *ooshunnawa* scrapes bottom against the sandy shore that once seemed so far away. Enrique and Akaiyan pull it far up upon the beach and run to lead the stallion and the two weary mares out of the water. The *a hots* are snorting with exhaustion and their legs are trembling.

"*Dámela,* give her to me," says Enrique, lifting the *yegüita* from the bottom of the canoe. With Akaiyan's help, they stand her upon the sand, rubbing her legs and her body. With a sudden bound she leaps free to run and join her mother. Even in her weakened state, the *bella yegua* sniffs and licks her baby. There is much snorting and cavorting around after that, with Enrique, Akaiyan and myself doing most of the dancing and running in circles. I never thought we'd make it across that wide expanse of water. I never thought the horses would make it, nor little Star. But we did! We crossed with God's help, with the love of the Great Spirit guiding us all the way. I kneel and give thanks to our Lord and Savior, Jesus Christ. Enrique kneels with me while Akaiyan stretches his arms heavenward, and we all pray.

Chapter 32

Croatoan Island

IT'S LATE WHEN WE MOUNT the horses again. We all needed the day to rest, *a hots* and humans. By evening, the horses have recovered well; the mares and stallion are grazing, the filly is suckling and seems none the worse for her experience. The sky is a dull winter grey when Enrique and Akaiyan tell me it's time to climb upon the brown mare. I do so with great eagerness, for surely we're on the last leg of our journey. Akaiyan springs upon his mare with ease. He's becoming a true *caballero*. Enrique has a difficult time with the black stallion, who's recovered his strength and seems anxious to race. He paws the sand and snorts with fervor, chomping the metal bit, trying to seize it between his teeth. Sand flies in all directions.

We head southeast once more as evening descends. I'm now so used to riding at night, the darkness doesn't scare me as it once did. Enrique keeps the black under tight rein, for he would gallop off and leave us behind if he could. The

127

yegüita trots willingly after her mother, and we all canter at a sharp pace.

Mile after mile, the ground is swallowed up under our *a hots'* hooves. We've left the *ooshunnawa* behind, for it's far too awkward to carry now that we ride the horses. I'm wondering how we'll cross the small channel of water which separates Croatoan Island, thinking of Star and what almost happened to her. Akaiyan says that we'll find a way.

We cover as much ground as we can, at the same time stopping often enough for Star to rest and feed. We move with a light heart, for the end is in sight. It's been a long and arduous journey with many dangers. Riding upon the *bella yegua*, my thoughts are now upon our return home, what my mother and father will say, what Manteo will do, how Eleanor will react when we tell her we couldn't bring Ananyas's body with us. Part of me is thrilled with anticipation at seeing my beloved Mother and Father again; another part is sorely afraid of what Manteo might say or do. I'm torn in two directions.

We reach the southernmost shoreline after several nights, riding down with the sea to our left, the sound to our right. At the farthest strip of land, where sound meets sea, we pull up our horses and dismount. All of us are exhausted. We tether the animals, for they're clearly in need of rest. I stare out at the water, seeing the trees of Croatoan Island just across the narrow channel, beckoning me, luring me onward.

It seems but a short distance after our last crossing, but here the waters are much more dangerous. The sea's tides pull at the placid sound, creating eddies and shifting sands beneath the surface. The sailor's greatest fear lies out beyond this shoreline; those treacherous shoals upon which many a ship has been dashed. Akaiyan calls these waters a false illusion, though there's not really an English translation for what he wants to say. It appears that one could almost walk across but then, one false step and the ocean floor drops away. Down, down you go, tugged in all directions.

"*Unqua* have... drowned," he tells me.

"How will we get Star across?"

"I will think on it."

I watch him pacing the sand. Enrique sits by me.

"I could try," he ventures. "*Yo soy un buen nadador.*"

I shake my head.

"Not that good a swimmer. We came across on the *ooshunnawa*. It took all of Akaiyan's and Skotai's strength to guide it. No one could swim, not even you."

After a while, Akaiyan goes into the trees near the shore. He comes back carrying some branches. I watch as he bends and shapes the soft wood, tying pieces together much like the harness for Star's head.

"I will float behind this and kick my feet. Then I won't sink."

"You can't. The tide will sweep you out to sea."

"I am strong. I will do it when the tide comes in."

But I'm sore afraid. I remember the stories of the rip tide at its worst, when the men returned from their fishing expedition to the outer coast. They told how several were almost swept away in the current, and only the efforts of the others saved them.

Then Enrique suggests that we light a fire instead, making lots of smoke which will surely attract someone on the other side. We can signal them to send many *ooshunnawa* to our rescue.

"The *utchar* will tell others where we are, too. The hunting parties of our enemies may be on these shores. They will see the flames and smoke."

With Akaiyan's warning, now we don't know what to do, swim or build a fire. The night is closing down upon us again and we need to sleep.

"We will rest here," says Enrique, feeding the *a hots* the last handfuls of grain. "But then, tomorrow, we must decide."

He's worried, I can tell, for their ribs are beginning to stick out from their hard ride and lack of proper food.

"We must find oats and hay for them," he says to Akaiyan. "Do the *unqua* have these things?"

After I translate, Akaiyan nods.

"We have much grain," he says, "and *oonaha,* corn as well."

I give Star a kiss on her soft nose, stroking her forehead. Then I hug the *bella yegua,* pat the other mare and approach the black. He stamps a hoof in the sand, then lowers his head for me to scratch between his ears.

"Diablo," I whisper. "You made such a good babe in Star. You're strong and powerful and she will be, too."

He snorts into my hand, trying to nibble my fingers.

"I have nothing to feed you," I say sorrowfully. "But tomorrow, you will have lots of *unqua* corn, I promise."

Chapter 33

Safe At Last

WE'RE AWAKENED in the morning by loud shouts. At first, I think it's Weapemeoc who've surrounded us, and my heart leaps in my breast. Akaiyan jumps to his feet, *oosocke nauh* in hand. Enrique pulls a firearm from his saddle pack, a weapon I didn't know he had.

"*¿Dónde están ellos?*" he whispers to me. "*Yo no veo a nadie.*"

It's true! There are no hostiles surrounding us, nor Spanish *soldados*. Then I see. Across the water, on the beach of Croatoan Island, *unqua* and *nickreruroh* are running up and down, pointing to us. It's impossible to see who they are and, I imagine, they can't know us. What a surprising sight we must be, an enemy perhaps, with horses!

"We have to signal and let them know who we are," I tell Akaiyan. "Remember, the men have firearms. They mustn't fire upon us."

I run to the water's edge and wade in up to my waist. The

tug of the tide grips my legs, threatening to pull me in further.

"Hello," I call as loudly as I can. "It's me, Jess. Hello, hello!" I'm waving my arms frantically back and forth.

"Akaiyan," he calls, wading in next to me. "We have returned. *Oon est nonne it quost!*"

At first, I don't know if they've understood. I'm squinting in the bright sunlight, which is spreading across the water from the horizon. Akaiyan suddenly bends and lifts me high in the air. I wave furiously. All of a sudden, several *ooshunnawa* are pushed into the water, and I can see men in them.

"They must know we're friends," I run to tell Enrique. "They must know!"

It seems to take forever for the *ooshunnawa* to cross. The tide is against them, going out toward the sea, so the canoes are difficult to maneuver. As they get closer, I can see Manteo in one, and my father, and Roger Bayley. I keep waving and waving....

The excitement that surrounds us is too much for Enrique, who hangs back with the *a hots*. The black stallion is nervous with all the people around, talking, laughing, hugging me.

"Oh, Jess," Father says over and over. "Oh, my darling Jess...."

He's overcome with such emotion that he can't talk any longer. A coughing fit seizes him and he's wracked with spasms. But he soon recovers enough to take me in his arms and hug me until my bones will surely break. I'm weeping from sheer joy. Even Manteo is glad to see us, though I know there will be much stern talk between him and Akaiyan later.

When they first see Enrique in his torn Spanish uniform, several of the men pull their firearms.

"No," I shout. "He's our friend. He helped us escape."

Then Father strides over to Enrique and embraces him.

"If you saved my beloved daughter, then you're welcome here."

Enrique is embarrassed and overwhelmed to see so many English, so many Indians in one place. He turns to the horses, to keep them calm.

The *unqua* hang back also, gasping in amazement at the *a hots*. Akaiyan speaks rapidly, trying to explain what they are and where they came from. I see him telling Manteo that they're nothing to be afraid of. To prove his point, he jumps upon the brown mare's back and gallops her up and down the beach. Manteo approaches hesitantly, then reaches out to pet Star. A faint smile appears on his face.

"We must go," he says then. "But how will we get the *a hots* in the *ooshunnawa?*"

And so we relive our sojourn across the water, Star in the canoe with me and Enrique, the other horses swimming behind, tethered by *utsera* as the men paddle. The tide has now turned and the pull of the water less strong. Even the mares are able to swim safely across.

My dear Mother is by the beach as we pull the canoes up upon the shore. She can't talk but just hugs me, tears running down her cheeks. Thomas is bouncing up and down, asking so many questions that my head's spinning.

"Where's Eleanor?" I ask Father, holding his hand as we walk back to the village.

"Waiting for you in her lodge house," he answers slowly. "Wondering if you've brought Ananyas home."

I shake my head sorrowfully. My father has already been told why we couldn't. He's silent for the rest of our journey.

Chapter 34

Message From George

"I UNDERSTAND," Eleanor whispers to me, "but my heart is heavy. I was so hoping...."

I just sit there holding her hand. Mother has taken little Virginia to our lodge house, while I try to explain to Eleanor about Ananyas's grave, the threat of the Weapemeoc, the Spanish *soldados*... everything.

"Did you say prayers over his body?"

"Yes, and over Master Spendlove, also."

"And my silver wedding band? Did you bury it above his heart?"

"Yes."

She weeps quietly, her eyes reddened and swollen. I'm at a loss for words.

"I read Our Lord's Prayer and the Twenty-Third Psalm," I say then, "and what Roger Prat had said, 'For earth thou art....' "

She kisses me gently on the cheek, rising to cross the

room, then pacing back and forth.

"Of course, you did what you could. It would have been... impossible to dig up... his... body...."

"The ground was frozen," I venture to say. "But I know I promised you... I'm so sorry."

She gives me a quick hug, then turns to stir her cooking pot.

"I must prepare dinner," she says, not looking at me. "The men brought me a portion of venison. I've not been wanting for food...."

Mother hasn't stopped showering me with kisses. She strokes my hair, my cheek, kissing me, touching me.

"I thought you were dead," she half-laughs, half-cries. "I didn't know where you were."

Throughout all this happy and sad time, Enrique has been an object of fascination. The English and the Indians haven't seen a Spanish *soldado* close up. The *unqua* touch his uniform, rubbing the gold embroidery of his jacket, the thick leather of his boots. The English men of our village are more reserved; Spain, after all, has been and still is our bitter enemy. Some of them can't understand how Enrique and I can be friends, even after I've explained it over and over again.

But it's the *a hots* that draw them all, *nickreruroh* and *unqua*. Manteo's people have never seen horses before. Like Akaiyan did in the beginning, they hang back, alarmed by every noise the horses make. The black stallion frets under such an audience, pawing the ground and snorting through flared nostrils, which quickly makes them run away. The *bella yegua* is nervous for her foal with too many humans around. She stamps her foot and lays back her ears. Again, they run. Only the other mare stands patiently, allowing the bravest of the *unqua quottis*, young men, to reach a tentative hand and stroke her sleek hide.

I overhear Akaiyan's brother, Quayah, tell him that the *a hots* are monsters, breathing fire and smoke from their noses. Akaiyan just laughs and leads Quayah to the mare, telling him to pet her on the nose and scratch behind her ears. When Quayah reaches out his hand, the mare lowers her head toward him. Quayah's face lights up, Akaiyan tells me later, and soon after he's begging his older brother to show him how to ride.

But the best discovery of all comes, not with the *a hots*, nor with Enrique, but with the rain-soaked, ink-smudged Bible that Enrique found in the deserted English settlement. I've told Father and the others about that colony, and they shake their heads in puzzlement as to what may have happened. We find the secret one day while I'm showing Eleanor the passages I read over the graves. As I thumb through the pages, a small piece of folded paper falls out from where it had been tucked, oh, so carefully, to keep it safe.

"What's this?" Eleanor asks, bending to pick up the paper.

"I never saw it before."

"There's writing on it."

Together we read the letter, while my heart beats faster and faster.

"In the hope that someone may find this, they must learn of the disaster which threatens. Powhatan's warriors are searching for us; even now, they move through the woodlands ever closer to our small camp. There was no Chesapeake Colony as we had supposed, but only ruins left smoldering and ravaged by fire. Half our brave colonists decided to stay and rebuild what had been destroyed. The others, along with myself, sought out a new settlement. Since that's endangered, we plan to move

inland, hoping for a different destiny. We will set fire to our encampment, leaving only ruins for the Savages to find, ourselves long gone before they arrive. We'll have the Cittie of Ralegh, as my father wished, even though it may not be at the Chesapeake Baye. In God's Most Holy Name, we pray for His protection and blessing upon our venture. Your faithful servant, George Howe."

"Oh, Eleanor," I gasp, tears running from my eyes. "George isn't dead. He's alive somewhere inland, far away from the coast."

"It's wondrous news," she exclaims, smiling for the first time in weeks. "Run and show this letter to your father and mother. Hurry now!"

But sobs consume me, so it's Eleanor who takes the letter to my beloved parents. Akaiyan comes and finds me crying.

"Little Bird," he asks, "are you sick?"

I shake my head.

"No, I'm happy."

But he doesn't understand. He stands bewildered until I explain, as best I can, what has caused my tears.

"Then why are you crying?" he questions, kissing my cheek.

"For joy," I answer. "For joy!"

Chapter 35

Inland Hopes

FATHER SAYS I HAVE a gift for language, and I suppose that's true. I'm now able to converse equally well in both Croatoan and Spanish. He tells me that I should become an ambassador for the *unqua*. I only laugh.

Akaiyan disappeared for three days. I found out later that Manteo disciplined him in the manner of the *unqua*, an isolation from the rest of the tribe for a set period of time. Akaiyan was given tasks to do and sent off into the woods surrounding the village, to contemplate his actions in taking me, a *nickreruroh*, into danger. I miss him terribly.

Today, Eleanor tells Mother and Father of her news, the forthcoming birth of her child.

"When is your confinement ended?" Mother asks, hugging her all the while.

"I'll deliver in July," she answers, then collapses in another fit of weeping upon my mother's shoulder.

"Hush, hush," Mother soothes. "This is a good thing.

Ananyas would be so happy."

"One life traded for another," Father says solemnly. "We'll pray for a boy child."

Already the babe moves within her womb, stirrings of life announcing its presence to the world. She holds her hands over her belly, half-smiling, half-melancholy. The child will be a blessing, Mother affirms. The women of the camp rally around her; Mistress Steueens comes with her hot tea and Wenefrid Powell, who gave birth just six months ago to a son, brings his baptismal clothes.

Father and Roger Bayley, along with several of the men, have questioned me in great detail about the Spanish garrison. I've told them everything I know. They wish to learn Spanish plans for conquests and settlements. But even Enrique can't answer their questions.

"I was only *un soldado*," he replies. "No one kept me informed. *Yo lo odiaba mientras estaba allí*, I hated it while I was there."

I can see the hatred on his face when he talks about the garrison. And I see the longing in his face for his *bella España*. How he misses his mother and sisters, almost as much as I missed my parents.

"You've no idea how beautiful it is," he tells me dreamily. "The sun shines all day long, the fields stretch out forever...."

But he's also a realist and turns his attentions toward the horses, whose needs are great. The other mare came into season and the black stallion has impregnated her. There'll be another foal in about ten months.

Star is filling out and growing. She suckles vigorously from the *bella yegua*, whom I've named Beauty. Whenever I'm not doing chores, or helping Eleanor, I'm at Beauty's side, grooming her, whispering secrets in her ear, playing with Star. Akaiyan calls me *kotchani a hots quirrera,* the one who loves horses.

Father speaks to me at great length about my ill-advised sojourn to the north.

"Though your intentions were honest," he says, "you placed yourself in great jeopardy. You were lucky to get away from the Spaniards. Your poor mother has been distraught with worry...."

"I couldn't have done it without Enrique," I tell him eagerly, explaining how the young *soldado* kept my secret and helped us escape. Father listens to my story, occasionally sighing, occasionally nodding his head.

"What should I do with such a daughter?" he asks, then reaches over to grab my hand. "We prayed every day and night for your safe return. God has surely answered our prayers."

He goes out to talk with Enrique. I can see them together, English and Spanish, standing near the horses. When he comes back, he gathers us together as a family.

"...Not all Spanish are our enemies," he says, looking directly at me and Thomas. "You must judge people by their actions, not their uniforms."

It's a lesson, of course, that I didn't need teaching, but I won't ever forget and neither will Thomas. Enrique has become his hero and Thomas his willing helper. The two of them, along with Akaiyan and Quayah, are always with the *a hots,* pampering them beyond belief.

Enrique is teaching Thomas and Quayah how to ride. Already they can race each other up and down the beach. The other *quottis* are eager to learn also. There's usually a crowd of young braves gathered around the animals. Star, especially, is the center of attention.

But the *nickreruroh* are in dissent, half of them wishing to move from Croatoan and head inland, half wanting to stay. There's talk about gathering our possessions once more and heading away from this island. Some of the men hope to find George and the others. It's just the way it was at Roanoak, with much talk and fervent discussion. Those who wish to search for George and the other colonists pour over John White's curled and ruined maps, seeking routes inland, making note of how many miles, pondering the dangers.

When questioned about the Chesapeake colonists who elected to remain, as George had written, I can only tell them that we saw no signs of anyone. Mother's heart is filled with a great sadness. No one knows what's happened to Dyonis or Margaret Harvye, or their babe Christopher.

Chapter 36

The Pledge

ALL DURING THE TIME I was imprisoned, I lost track of the days. It seems the year passed from 1588 to 1589, Thomas became thirteen and I, sixteen, without a celebration. Mother and Father have just given me one, complete with presents and singing. Mother gives me silver earrings that once belonged to her; Father gives me a book of poetry. Eleanor hands me one of her most precious possessions, a tiny golden lion dangling on a chain, given to her by Ananyas.

"Oh, I can't take such a beautiful thing."

"I want you to have it," she insists. "Ananyas told me once that if we had another child, he'd want it to be like you. He called you a little lioness."

"He did? Why?"

"Because you're strong at heart. How he admired your courage, your willingness to adapt to new surroundings! We often talked about it. I know he'd be pleased that I gave the lion to you."

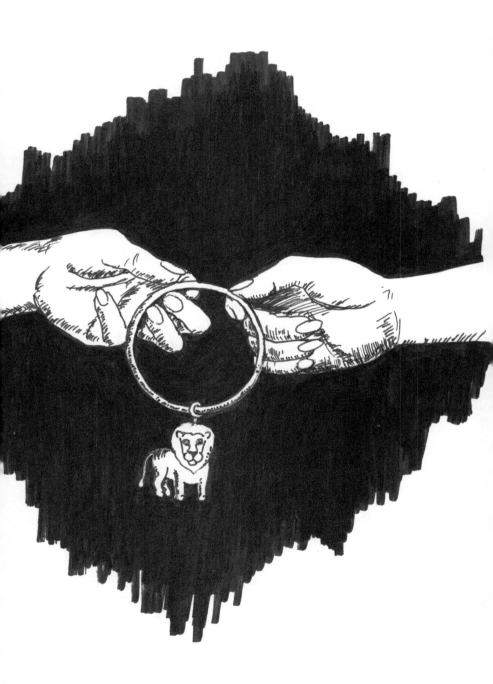

I hug her. She couldn't be more a sister to me than if we had the same parents. I keep fingering the tiny lion all in gold, his eyes two sparkling diamond chips.

"This must have cost a fortune."

"He told me there was no price on his love for me."

She turns away, trying hard not to cry.

"He saved many months to buy it. I told him he was foolish for spending his money like that, but he wanted me to have it."

"I'll treasure it always," I say then, kissing her cheek and running from the room, overcome with emotion. I can hear them singing as I walk across the village to where the *a hots* are safe and warm. Beauty whinnies low in her throat when she sees me. Star butts me with her head. Even Diablo snorts a greeting.

"I knew you'd come," Akaiyan says, stepping from the shadows. "I have a... special present for you."

Before I can say anything, he pulls me close, holding me, kissing me most passionately. I'm kissing him back with equal fervor. We sink down upon the cold ground and kiss some more. I can feel his hands moving, touching, soft as *oosnooqua*, feathers. Suddenly, I scramble to my feet.

"No... we can't... I mustn't...."

"Little Bird... I love you... I want to make you... my *kateocca*, wife."

My heart stops beating, then begins again, racing within my breast. There's nothing I want more.

"I want to marry you, too," I whisper. He places a leather thong with an amulet around my neck, then kisses me again.

"This is my pledge," he says. "I will go and ask your mother and father.... Is that not what the English do?"

I nod my head, filled both with excitement and a growing

fear. I want to be Akaiyan's wife with all my heart and soul. But I know Mother and Father won't approve. They feel that I'm too *unqua* now; certainly, they won't sanction my marriage to an Indian.

I watch him go, wishing this could be a happy time. I suddenly remember my friends back in England, Alice and Mary. If they brought a young man home, he'd be received with joyous cries and much fanfare. Why can't my betrothal be the same? But, of course, I already know the answer. My heart is torn between my love for Akaiyan and my wish to please my parents.

He's with them a long time, while I busy myself with Beauty and little Star. The filly is such a delight. I marvel at her slender legs, her brush of a tail, the deep luminescence of her eyes. She's growing so rapidly. I kiss her over and over, then lean my head against Beauty and close my eyes. I love the smell of the *a hots*, rich and full of the earth and sky. Not to ignore the others, I turn to the newly pregnant mare and hug her. She blows her warm breath into my hands.

"You need a name, too," I whisper, thinking of what I can call her.

"*Oorhast*, the swan. No, something better, *Oorhatha*, my little swan."

She flicks her tail and pushes her head against me.

"Little Swan, do you like your new name? You'll have a babe, just like Star. Are you pleased?"

Star is pushing against me, and I realize she wants to play. I'm so busy with the *a hots* that I don't notice Father is standing by the doorway.

"They love you," he comments, coughing slightly.

"I love them, too," I reply, turning to face him. "They carried us far away from the Spanish *soldados*. Akaiyan thought he was flying...."

Father's face is grim.

"I'm not happy in saying this, my dearest Jess, but you can't marry... an Indian."

"Why not?" I blurt out, then wish I'd held my tongue.

"Their ways are too different from ours. You must remember that you're English-born."

"But I love their ways, their gentleness. They're not like the hostiles who plunder and kill."

"Your mother and I were hoping...."

"...that I'd marry George Howe."

He sighs. "Possibly. Or another of your choosing."

"Akaiyan is of my choosing," I say stubbornly. He sighs again. I see in the fading light that my beloved father is looking old and tired. He holds out his arms to me and I go to him, weeping softly against his shoulder.

"We thought you dead. We almost lost hope. My dear..."

"I'm here, Father, and I love him so."

"We will see," he says then. "We will have to wait and see."

Chapter 37

Are You Werricauna?

MOTHER IS SILENT when I return to our lodge house. She busies herself with cleaning up the supper dishes, and shooing Thomas to get ready for bed. Father is still outside, though it's quite cold and I worry for him. Perhaps he's planned it this way, to give Mother time to talk with me.

"It's so strange," she says, "to see a Spanish boy here in our midst. He's quite a young man, not at all what I thought the enemy was like."

"Enrique isn't our enemy, dear Mother. He never was. He was forced into service by his uncle. And he never liked the idea of fighting. He's a farmer, and a lover of *a hots*."

She stares at me.

"I mean horses, *los caballos*. He loves them so much."

"You're quite fluent in his language, I see. You have a true gift that way."

"Spanish is a beautiful tongue, full of rhythm. I like the way it flows... but...."

"...You're also fluent in the language of our Indian friends. Dear Jess...," she comes over to me.

"Mother, please don't tell me not to love Akaiyan. For, indeed, I do love him very much. He's asked me to be his wife."

She sighs, then quickly wipes a tear from her eye. "You're more Indian than I thought. Your father and I have been beside ourselves with grief. We thought you'd been killed. We lived for the day you'd come back. And now here you are, and you want to... marry an Indian boy."

"Don't you like Manteo and his people?"

"Of course I do. It's taken me a while to get used to living this way, but they're all so good to us, how could I not like them? But that doesn't mean... I want you to marry one."

She's weeping now. Oh, I've seen so many tears lately, my own begin to flow as quickly as hers. I go to her and we hold each other.

"Mother, dearest Mother, I was almost dead and now I've come back to you. Please don't make me have to choose between you and Akaiyan."

Thomas comes bounding in, interrupting to say good night. He's grown so much, he's almost as tall as Father. I keep forgetting he's thirteen and becoming a man before my eyes. I go outside then and Father passes, giving me a quick kiss on the cheek. The night is cold, though spring will be upon us soon. I'll be so glad when this dreary winter season is ended.

Akaiyan is once more by the *a hots*, settling them down for the night. Enrique is playing with Star.

"My *bella yegua* has a sore foot," Enrique says, lifting up her leg and examining her hoof. "She must have stepped on *una pequeña piedra*."

I can see that the frog of the hoof is slightly swollen from the stone.

"What can you do?"

"I'll apply a poultice. It will not take long."

He's gone before I know it, leaving me alone with Akai-yan.

"I spoke with my parents. They're not happy."

He nods his head.

"I have yet to tell my father. I will wait until we're alone."

"Are you *werricauna?*"

"Perhaps, a little." He smiles. "And you?"

"Only when I'm away from you."

We kiss again. I lean my head against his shoulder.

"How do the *unqua* treat their *kateocca?*"

"We love our wives as the mothers of our children, the bearers of our seed, the ones from whom all life springs."

"Will I make a good *unqua* wife?"

"You will be like *heita* in my life, like the sun which shines on us all."

I hold him gently, kissing his eyes, his mouth.

"I love you so much. You're my sun, my moon. I won't let anything come between us."

"*Jureha,* I will speak with my father. *Jureha,* we will both go to your parents and tell them how much we love each other."

When Enrique comes back, we help him with Beauty. She lets us place the healing poultice on her hoof. Enrique ties it with a cloth. We watch as Star suckles, listening to the sounds she makes, hearing Diablo stamping on the ground, and Little Swan snorting as she eats. Beauty turns her head to stare at the three of us.

"What are you thinking, *bella yegua?*"

"She loves her foal."

"We all love her foal."

"Tomorrow, her foot will be better," Enrique says then. "And tonight I will sleep here, close by her side."

Chapter 38

Final Decision

AFTER ABOUT THREE DAYS of discussion, Richard Wildye, Christopher Cooper, and several of the others came before all of us to propose leaving Croatoan Island.

"We can't give up hope of finding our friends. We can never give up hope!"

"No one knows where they are," Mother interrupts.

"Nevertheless, we can guess their general route. After all, like us, they saw John White's maps back on Roanoak. We can try to follow where they might have gone. It's a chance we should take."

"And find nothing!" Mistress Steueens states angrily. "Just like there was nothing left at Chesapeake. Or worse, be killed...."

"Hush, woman," Master Steueens says. "We must listen to what they have to say."

I can't bear to be around. For I know in my heart of hearts, that I will never leave Croatoan Island to search again for an

English colony. Better not to know where they are, to imagine them still alive, than to stumble upon the truth: a ruined settlement, houses burned to the ground, crosses marking the graves of fallen friends. I leave the lodge house after that, going to where the *a hots* are, for with them I find peace and tranquility.

When I return home, Mother and Father are earnestly discussing our future.

"Your Mother wants to go this time," Father says, "but I can't travel any more."

"We know how you feel, dear Jess, but the truth is, we can't remain here any longer."

"Why not?"

"Because we're outstaying our welcome. And the children, all of them, are turning into Indians before our very eyes."

I can feel the tears behind my eyes, but I can't, I won't cry. Indian women are more reserved than their English counterparts. I swallow deeply and hold my head up high.

"Dearest Mother, Father, even if you decide to leave Croatoan, I'll stay. For my heart's here with Akaiyan, with all the *unqua*."

They stare at me, not a word between them. There's nothing they can say, after all, that will change my mind.

That evening, in her fifth month of confinement, Eleanor goes into premature labor. Contractions begin and she suffers all day and night, finally bringing forth from her womb a dead boy child.

Sometimes, I wonder if the eyes can stand any more tears, if they can deal with the copious outpouring of salty water. How red can they become, how puffy and swollen, before the lids must burst and the eyes fall from their sockets? In truth,

I've no more tears left. For to see Eleanor labor so, crying out in pain and anguish because she knows that it's too early, that her child, her last remembrance of Ananyas, can only be dead, is too much to bear.

Mother rushes to and fro, summoning Mistress Steueens, Wenefrid Powell, anyone she can think who might be of help. Eleanor had complained of some cramping and so, she'd wisely gone to bed for the past few days. Then staining appeared and finally, an outpouring of blood and the actual pains of labor. When at last it ended, a bloody mixture of membrane and tissue was her only reward, a perfectly formed boy child, Mother sobbed, but too small to save.

The dead babe was taken away and buried in a corner of the burial ground which the *unqua* have given us, a place we've consecrated. Prayers were said and everybody cried. Eleanor stayed resting at our lodge house, too weak and overcome with this newest grief to attend.

"Our first burial on this island," Mother weeps.

"But not our first," Mistress Steueens sobs, remembering Agnes, John Tydway, George Howe the elder, and our two most recent, Ananyas and Master Spendlove.

"Our numbers dwindle down," Mother says. "This new babe would have blessed us all."

"Oh, Mother, I'll have many children," I cry out. "I want lots."

She turns to me then, her face a mask of pain and sorrow. But she can't speak any words, collapsing into tears. Father takes her arm and guides her away. The others leave soon after. Only I'm left, to stand in the morning sun and stare at the small cross and the freshly-turned earth.

A week later, Eleanor gets up from her bed of sorrows and announces that she'll go with those who want to leave.

"There's nothing for me here," she says, a firmness in her tone which surprises all of us.

"But what of little Virginia?"

"She comes with me. Together, we'll seek out a new life for ourselves. We'll find George and the others. Jess, will you come with us?"

But I shake my head, while Mother weeps anew.

"No, my home is here."

"Then come with us part-way. Be our guide out of these wretched banks. You, Enrique and Akaiyan know the land. Help us on our way."

She's gripping my hands until they turn white. I nod my head.

"No, Jess," Mother exclaims, "we're staying here. I've decided. Your father isn't well enough to undergo such a journey, and I won't leave him. We're staying here with you. You mustn't go."

"Only part-way, Mother, until they're safely off the banks. Then we'll come back."

I stare at her, at Father, at them both, my parents whom I love with all my heart. Though I can understand why Eleanor must leave this place, for there's not even a grave where she can mourn Ananyas, my heart belongs with the *unqua*. I sense Akaiyan's hand slipping into mine. I can see Enrique watching us, standing close to *los caballos* he loves.

"We'll lead you out," I say then with assurance, "until you reach the mainland. Then we'll return. My heart is here, my life is here."

And in front of Mother and Father, I turn to Akaiyan and draw him close, to hold him and kiss him without fear or shame.

Epilogue

HISTORIANS DISAGREE as to what may have happened during the three years that John White was forced to remain in England, unable to return with men and supplies.

One theory is that the men and women who headed north, the Chesapeake Colonists, were massacred by Powhatan's war-like tribes. Another theory entertains the fact that Eleanor Dare and a small group may have left the sanctuary of Croatoan Island and traveled inland, eventually reaching what is now Georgia.

Spanish explorers, ranging inland, brought their horses with them. The Indians, no doubt, thought the beasts with their riders were monsters. Some Indians killed and ate the captured animals. Others, discovering the wonders of such swift creatures, learned how to tame them and ride like the wind.

The Lyon Saga explores all these possibilities.

**Jess's adventures continue in the third book of
The Lyon Saga...**

The Lyon's Pride

When Eleanor Dare and some of the other colonists decide
to head inland, Jess, Akaiyan and Enrique volunteer to
lead them part way. The journey takes them through
dangerous territory where more adventures lie in store.
Will they be able to return home safely to Croatoan Island,
and what awaits them there?

THE NAMES OF THE 1587 VIRGINIA COLONISTS

THE names of all the men, women and Children, which safely arrived in Virginia, and remained to inhabite there. 1587.

Anno Regni Reginae Elizabethae .29.

John White [Governor]
Roger Bailie [Assistant]
Ananias Dare [Assistant]
Christopher Cooper [Assistant]
Thomas Stevens [Assistant]
John Sampson [Assistant]
Dyonis Harvie [Assistant]
Roger Prat [Assistant]
George Howe [Assistant]
Simon Fernando [Assistant]
Nicholas Johnson
Thomas Warner
Anthony Cage
John Jones
John Tydway
Ambrose Viccars
Edmond English
Thomas Topan
Henry Berrye
Richard Berrye
John Spendlove
John Hemmington
Thomas Butler
Edward Powell
John Burden

James Hynde
William Willes
John Brooke
Cutbert White
John Bright

Clement Tayler
William Sole
John Cotsmur
Humfrey Newton
Thomas Colman
Thomas Gramme
Marke Bennet
John Gibbes
John Stilman
Robert Wilkinson
Peter Little
John Wyles
Brian Wyles
George Martyn
Hugh Pattenson
Martyn Sutton
John Farre
John Bridger

Griffen Jones
Richard Shaberdge
Thomas Ellis
William Brown
Michael Myllet
Thomas Smith
Richard Kemme
Thomas Harris
Richard Taverner
John Earnest
Henry Johnson
John Starte
Richard Darige
William Lucas
Arnold Archard
John Wright
William Dutton
Morris Allen
William Waters
Richard Arthur
John Chapman
William Clement
Robert Little
Hugh Tayler
Richard Wildye
Lewes Wotton
Michael Bishop
Henry Browne
Henry Rufoote
Richard Tomkins
Henry Dorrell

Charles Florrie
Henry Mylton
Henry Payne
Thomas Harris
William Nicholes
Thomas Phevens
John Borden
Thomas Scot
James Lasie
John Cheven
Thomas Hewet
William Berde

Women

Elyoner Dare
Margery Harvie
Agnes Wood
Wenefrid Powell
Joyce Archard
Jane Jones
Elizabeth Glane
Jane Pierce
Audry Tappan
Alis Chapman
Emme Merrimoth
Colman
Margaret Lawrence
Joan Warren
Jane Mannering
Rose Payne
Elizabeth Viccars

The Names of the 1587 Virginia Colonists

Boyes and Children
John Sampson
Robert Ellis
Ambrose Viccars
Thomas Archard
Thomas Humfrey
Tomas Smart
George Howe
John Prat
William Wythers

Children born in Virginia
Virginia Dare
Harvye

Savages
Manteo ⎫ That were in Englande and returned home
Towaye ⎭ into Virginia with them.

FURTHER READING

Daniell, David, Editor. *Tyndale's New Testament*. New Haven & London: Yale University Press, 1989.

————. *Tyndale's Old Testament*. New Haven & London: Yale University Press, 1989.

Durant, David N. *Ralegh's Lost Colony: The Story of the First English Settlement in America*. New York: Atheneum, 1981.

Hoffman, Paul E. *Spain and the Roanoke Voyages*. Raleigh: North Carolina Dept. of Cultural Resources, Division of Archives and History, 1987.

Humber, John L. *Backgrounds and Preparations for the Roanoke Voyages, 1584-1590*. Raleigh: North Carolina Dept. of Cultural Resources, Division of Archives and History, 1986.

Kupperman, Karen Ordahl. *Roanoke, The Abandoned Colony*. Maryland: Rowman and Littlefield, 1984.

Lawson, John. *A New Voyage to Carolina*. Chapel Hill: University of North Carolina, 1967.

Miller, Helen Hill. *Passage to America: Ralegh's Colonists Take Ship for Roanoke*. Raleigh: North Carolina Dept. of Cultural Resources, Division of Archives and History, 1983.

Perdue, Theda. *Native Carolinians: The Indians of North Carolina*. Raleigh: North Carolina Dept. of Cultural Resources, Division of Archives and History, 1985.

Quinn, David Beers. *The Lost Colonists: Their Fortune and Probable Fate*. Raleigh: North Carolina Dept. of Cultural Resources, Division of Archives and History, 1984.

———. *Set Fair For Roanoke: Voyages and Colonies, 1584-1606*. Chapel Hill: University of North Carolina Press, 1985.

Quinn, David B. & Alison Quinn. *The First Colonists: Documents on the Planting of the First English Settlements In North America, 1584-1590*. Raleigh: North Carolina Dept. of Cultural Resources, Division of Archives and History, 1982.

Rights, Douglas L. *The American Indian in North Carolina*. Winston-Salem: John F. Blair, 1991.

Stick, David. *Roanoke Island: The Beginnings of English America*. Chapel Hill: University of North Carolina, 1983.